HAUNTED INDIANA 4

Mark Marimen

Introduction by Lee Lavery

Holt, Michigan

Printed in the United States of America

ISBN: 1-933272-05-8

Cover photograph by Chris Shultz

Cover design by Adventures with Nature, East Lansing, Michigan

Other titles in the Thunder Bay Press *Tales of the Supernatural* series:

Haunted Indiana (by Mark Marimen)
Haunted Indiana 2 (by Mark Marimen)
Haunted Indiana 3 (by Mark Marimen)
School Spirits (by Mark Marimen)
Chicagoland Ghosts
Haunts of the Upper Great Lakes
Michigan Haunts and Hauntings

Audio CD Information:

Recorded Live at "The Coffee Beanery," Dyer, Indiana, April 2005.

Recorded and mastered by Don Bernacki

CONTENTS

DEDICATION

This book is lovingly dedicated to the memory of my father,
Wilfred G. Wilkins

The one who sees the furthest is the one who stands on the shoulders of a giant.

Thanks for being my giant.

ACKNOWLEDGEMENTS AND THANKS...

Although it is almost passé to note in the acknowledgements of such works, this book truly has been made possible through the help of a great many people. I am deeply grateful to all who gave of their time, energy and talent in its research and writing.

Thanks are due to my wife and daughter, who have put up with a husband and father who at moments has been preoccupied with the writing of this book.

Special thanks are due to my friend and fellow writer Lee Lavery, whose words introduce this work. I hope you remember this when you write your bestseller.

Thanks also to some very talented people who have helped polish and edit this work, including Bill and Patty Wilkins, and Ms. Julie Stucky, a great editor in the making. Your time and efforts are something I have treasured.

Thanks are also due to those who have helped in the research in this work, specifically Kathy Harlow, who provided generously from her stockpile of ghostly tales, as well as dear friends Don and Laura Bernacky for their expertise and advice. Thanks to the staffs of the Johnson County Museum of History, the Old County Jail Museum, and Franklin College for their invaluable aid. Thanks also to Ben Hinton, for his aid in information of Free Masonry.

Thanks to all who accompanied me on this journey, including Doug Johns and Steve Conger, as well as Abigail Wilkins, whose company on my travels made them worth the while. Thanks to my photographer and one of my oldest friends, Chris Shultz, who donated his time and considerable photographic skill.

Thanks to my staff, especially Theresa, who supported me during the time necessary to do this task.

Thanks to Dr. Douglas Zale, M.D., who once told me I could do this, long before I thought I could.

Finally a sincere debt of thanks is recognized to all who trusted me with their stories. It is a privilege that I hope I have lived up to.

INTRODUCTION

Lee Lavery

The 1960s and 1970s in Northwest Indiana was a good time and place to be a kid. Being a kid in Northwest Indiana meant playing tag, building forts under Grandma's willow tree, and telling ghost stories. If you grew up in Northwest Indiana back then, you knew that ghost stories were a part of every slumber party, every bonfire, and every late September evening as you felt the summer's warmth begin to ebb and the bite of autumn steal into the air. Stories of pale women dressed in white flowing dresses standing by the side of the road and of the man who spent eternity searching for his golden arm made us dive under our beds, vow never to go into the basement again, and beg to sleep with the lights on. Scary? Yes. Occasionally irritating to our parents? Yes. A rite of passage? Absolutely!

Mark Marimen embraced this rite of passage as a child—and still embraces it. All you have to do is sit in the quiet of a cool autumn night and read his tales of Indiana ghosts, and you too will feel the magic take hold. The delight of a shiver brought on by specters and things that go bump in the night, the youthful joy of feeling goosebumps creep up your arm as a shadow floats past your peripheral vision. The curiosity about happenings for which there is simply no good answer are the feelings Mark Marimen knows and describes in his stories.

While many have written horrific tales of anguished souls fraught with eternal suffering and unending remorse, Marimen seeks out and writes about those stories that inspire excitement and trepidation. Since he cares about the history and legends of his hosts, Marimen is able to tell their stories with the affection of a friend, completely and wholly because he is never content to simply tell the 'gory details.' Marimen has a fondness for his ghosts, and that feeling bubbles over into his writing and leaves us with a sense of childlike glee. Reading Mark's stories is like having an open window into our youth, and that window gives us a chance to set aside the daily responsibilities and stresses of adulthood to, once again, be that child hiding under the bed and loving every spine-tingling minute of it.

Mark generously shares the magic and wonder that ghost stories brought to his youth. A quickened pulse, the feeling that someone is watching you, and just a bit of childhood magic is part of what Mark brings to his writing. He has held on to the magic and kept it safe from the cynicism maturity sometimes brings. He has allowed it to grow with him into adulthood, and it is that magic and sense of wonder, that innocent enchantment, that shines through in his stories. So come now, sit back, dim the lights (but not too low), and allow Mark to walk with you for just a while…back to the simplicity and abandon of your youth through the magic of the book you hold in your hands.

PREFACE

(A good time for a ghost story)

Writing this preface is a bit of a break with tradition for me. In writing my last four collections of ghost stories, it has been my tradition to save the writing of the introduction for Halloween night, feeling it an appropriate time for such an endeavor. However, as I sit alone tonight by the light of my desk lamp, the calendar on the wall tells me it is January, and the cold wind whistling past my eaves, dropping the temperature to nearly zero confirms the fact. A part of me seems at odds with writing an introduction during this, the bleakest time of the year, when reality and "normality" grasps life in its chilly claw. Yet, I must admit that another part of me feels that it is right, and even appropriate to save the writing of this introduction for a night such as this.

My mind returns to a short conversation I had several months ago, and the thoughts that it prompted. It started in mid October with a phone call from an acquaintance from church, who had just found out that I was the same Mark Marimen who wrote "those Indiana ghost books." While such a discovery has been known to raise an eyebrow or two, in this case she was delighted. She asked if I might have time to come to her daughter's Girl Scout troop and share some ghost stories at their Halloween meeting the next week. Somewhat regretfully, I was forced to tell her that since October is "prime time" for an author of ghost stories, my schedule was solidly booked for the next few weeks, but suggested that I might be available in November or the coming months to entertain her daughter's troop. For her part, she assured me she understood, but then added, "I'm not sure that coming next month will work. After all, Halloween is the time for ghost stories, isn't it?"

While I understood her reply, as I later revisited the conversation in my mind, I found myself asking, "Just when *is* the right time for ghost stories?" It has become a fascinating question for me as I have reflected on it.

Of course, my caller had a good point. Autumn, and particularly the Halloween season, is the time we most often associate with tales of the supernatural. There is little as delicious as settling down underneath a red harvest moon, with the wind rustling among the leaves to share a good ghostly tale. There is something about the very atmosphere of late autumn, as the darkness grows and the air grows damp and cool as the tomb that draws us to the eerie side of life. Perhaps it is no coincidence that Halloween, the time when legends says the veil between this world and the next is at its most transparent, is celebrated at this time of the year. But is this the only truly fitting time for a ghost story?

Surely other seasons too, have their claim as apropos settings for ghost stories. Summer, too, serves well as a venue for such tales. As I related in an earlier introduction, it was sitting by a campfire during my twelfth summer that I received my first real introduction to ghost stories. Since writing of this part of my youth, I have come to discover a host of others who have similar memories. There is something about a summer campfire, as it sheds its feeble light against the darkness and the stars slowly fade into existence overhead, which makes tales of the unquiet dead seem real to us. Perhaps this is because it is in such a setting that we share the experience of our primordial ancestors, who first sat around their fires and whispered tales of a world they understood even less than we understand ours. The hush of a summer night and the crackle of a campfire make up a truly classic setting for the sharing of ghost stories.

Spring also holds a certain charm of the aficionado of ghostly tales. Specifically, warm spring nights when the thunder rolls and lightning pierces the sky are perfect for such endeavors. It is in the spring that nature is at its most violent, and most dramatic. As wind lashes the rain against the window pane and the full moon is obliterated by ominous clouds, it is easy to have one's thoughts turn to the macabre. Indeed, it was on just such a spring evening by the shores of Lake Geneva that a young woman named Mary Shelley put pen to paper to begin the story that would become the book *Frankenstein*. Were it not for the drama afforded by that spring night, the world might have been deprived of one of its most classic supernatural tales.

Certainly, good arguments can be made for the appropriateness of spring, summer and fall for the sharing of ghost stories, but what about that most banal of all seasons, winter? It is true that Dickens chose Christmas as the setting for his classic *A Christmas Carol*, yet despite this notable exception winter hardly seems to provide a genial setting for ghost stories, particularly in the Midwest. Indeed, it seems that there is little more grindingly "real" than midwinter in Indiana. When the frigid wind roars across an Indiana farm field (in a direct trajectory from the Arctic Circle), winter is driven deep into our Hoosier souls, leaving no room for anything as whimsical as a world where specters lurk. As the world slumbers in winter's icy embrace, there is little to draw on the fanciful or romantic facets of our nature. In short, winter is a time when the normal and mundane hold sway.

Yet, oddly, perhaps it is these very characteristics that make for the *perfect* occasions for ghost stories for me. At the very least, it is the very times when life is at its most mundane that I feel the greatest appreciation for the lure of ghostlore.

As I have often commented, ghost stories, for me, are all about the magic and romance of our world. Existing in the dim netherworld between the sterile reality of our everyday existence and the safety of utter fiction, ghost stories exist to remind us that perhaps there is more to our world than is readily apparent. Ghost stories keep their magic, in part, precisely because they pose the unanswerable questions of life and death, and draw us away from our commonplace existence and into a world of wonder and imagination.

So, perhaps it's appropriate that I sit here alone on a cold winter night, with the chill wind battering my window pane, and write the introduction to my fifth collection of ghostly stories. It has now been more than seven years since I accidentally fell into the world of writing ghost stories, and in that time I have come to have a renewed love of, and appreciation for, the otherworldly side of our state. I remain deeply grateful to all who have shared these tales with me, and I count it a privilege to be able to collect and retell them.

I hope that this volume will, once more, entertain you, and perhaps even chill you. However, more than this, it is my hope that these tales reacquaint you of the wonder and magic that still lies beneath the veneer of our rational world. In any case, this is a volume for those moments when life seems all too grindingly real, and what is needed is a visit to a world where spirits lurk. In other words, a time...*just like this.*

The magic beckons, and the spirits await. Let the tales begin.

Mark Marimen
January 10, 2005

"There are more things in heaven and earth, Horatio,
Than are dreamt of in your philosophy."

William Shakespeare

In the writing of this book, careful attention has been given to collecting legends that in many instances have been told for generations. In some cases, scenes have been recreated in the telling of these old legends that might not reflect exact historical events. The author makes no claim as to the exact historical authenticity of any of the legends represented in this book. Additionally, some of those who have chosen to tell their stories in this book have requested that their names be changed to protect their privacy. In these cases, an asterisk (*) follows the name the first time it is mentioned.

1
A GRANDFATHER'S TALE

It can be seen that Indiana, no less than any state of our nation, seems to have its share of tales of ghosts and apparitions. Some are dark, macabre legends of lurking phantoms and gloomy specters. Many others, however, are of a more benign and even gentle nature.

Such is the story told by Marie McBee,* a registered nurse who resides in south central Indiana. Hers is a story of great personal import and reflection. Far from the common stuff of ghostlore, it is a tender story from her history that still gives her peace today. In the end, it may not be a ghost story at all, but instead, a story about family and the power of love.

As Marie relates her story, she was born near Pittsburgh, where she lived for the first six years of her life. Without going into detail, she expresses that her time there was happy, filled with friends and laughter.

Her childhood, and a bit of her innocence, was shattered by two events that occurred just after her sixth birthday. The first was the divorce of her parents, followed closely by her father moving out of the state. The second came about a month or so later when Marie's mother came into her bedroom, sat on the end of her bed, and as gently as she could, told Marie that the two of them would be moving to her hometown in Indiana. Understandably, Marie was devastated by the news; she didn't want to leave her home, her friends, and her school.

Marie's mother explained that since the divorce she had been looking for employment but had been unable to find any work. Just that week, however, a friend from her hometown had offered her a job in a factory in Oldenburg. The job would provide the pair with a livable income to care for their needs. Besides, she reminded Marie, her father (Marie's grandfather) was now living alone in a small house in the country just outside Oldenburg, and he could "use some looking after." It would also give Marie a chance to get to know her grandpa, who she had only met a couple of times on their infrequent visits to Indiana. Grandpa even offered to let them live in the old family home, jut an eighth of a mile up the road from his house for free.

Needless to say, all of this did little to make Marie feel better about the move. She barely remembered her grandpa, and the prospect of moving from a nice suburban neighborhood to the countryside of Indiana did not sound inviting.

Still, in another month, both mother and daughter packed all their belongings into a moving van and headed west. They settled into their new old home, and life began anew. As Marie remembers, however, it was a dark and lonely time for her at first, despite her new surroundings. They lived on a secluded country road with no immediate neighbors, and thus no other children in the area for her to befriend. Since they had moved in the early summer, it would be months until Marie would go to school and meet others of her age, and there was little for her to do to occupy her time.

Even being near her grandpa was no consolation at first. In fact, Marie admits to being somewhat intimidated by the old man. Today she describes him as a large man with bushy eyebrows and a scraggly white beard. His hands were gnarled and callused from years of hard work, and in his mouth there was always a pipe, its rich, aromatic smoke curling past his mustache. He smoked the pipe from morning till night, and the knotty pine paneling of his small home seemed embedded with the smell. Though polite, Marie remembers him to be a little reserved at first, as though he was as intimidated by her as she was by him.

However, as days turned to weeks, their relationship began to warm. It started with a small toy left by her dinner plate one evening. When Marie's mother asked where it came from, Grandpa innocently exclaimed that the fairies must have left it. That night Marie's hug was just a little warmer and lingered for a moment longer than usual.

A courtship of sorts began between the two. With a gentle smile and a teasing comment, they began to feel a little more comfortable with each other. Marie fondly remembers the moment that cemented their relationship. One day about a month after she moved into her new home, Marie and her mother were at her grandpa's, as had become their afternoon custom. Her mother was in the kitchen preparing dinner while Marie was in the front yard playing. As she came running into the front room, hurrying to show her mother the flowers she had just picked, her elbow brushed an antique lamp next to the easy chair where her grandpa was sitting.

As she watched, horrified, the lamp tottered for a split second and then crashed to the floor, shattering. In a moment her mother came running from the kitchen, a wrath in her eyes that only a parent can muster, demanding to know what had happened. Before Marie could gasp out a reply, she heard Grandpa say, "What happened? I'll tell ya. I was reaching for my pipe tobacco and bumped the darn lamp. Oh well, it was an old thing anyway, and I've been meaning to replace it."

From that moment on, the two were close friends. Every morning that summer, Marie and her mother would rise early, get dressed, and walk the eighth of a mile down the country road, past the small country cemetery along the way, to Grandpa's for breakfast. When they arrived, they would inevitably find that Grandpa was already up and ensconced in his easy chair with the morning paper on his lap before him, smoking his morning pipe, the smoke rich and delicious in the air.

Marie's mother would immediately proceed to the kitchen to prepare breakfast while, with a smile and a wink, Grandpa would open his arms and Marie would fly onto his lap. Together the two would read the paper, taking turns reading articles to one another and laughing at the comics.

When school started, Marie found that she liked her teacher and made some new friends, but it was her grandpa who was the light of her life. That fall her mother announced to Marie that she had received a promotion at work. While this would further help their family, it also meant that she would have to work later into the afternoon shift, sometimes not getting home until six or seven o'clock. However, this presented no problem for Marie or her grandpa. Now when the school bus dropped Marie off in front of her grandpa's house, she would fly in to tell him all about her day, and then the two would go into the kitchen and make supper together. Marie recalls with a smile that her grandpa was not much of a cook, but somehow macaroni and cheese or hotdogs and beans tasted like a feast when she and her grandpa had made the meal together.

When supper was over and the dishes washed, the pair would go back into the living room where Grandpa would start a fire in the fireplace. Marie would stretch out in front of the fire with her schoolbooks around her, doing her homework. Sometimes, when she had finished her schoolwork, Marie would sit by the firelight and listen, entranced, to her grandpa tell stories about what life had been like when he was growing up in Indiana.

Occasionally, in the early spring or fall, storms would blow up out of the west, and Marie, who was deathly afraid of storms, would instinctively fly into her grandpa's lap. As she shivered, listening to the thunder roar, he would gently take his gnarled hand and pat the back of her head. "It's OK, honey, you're safe," he would gently murmur. "The storm will pass, and I'm right here. You don't think I would ever let anything happen to you, do you?" And slowly Marie would feel her trembling pass, her fears swallowed up in the warmth of her grandpa's love.

This blissful existence lasted for almost four years before Marie's world was once again shattered. Grandpa got sick. He went to the hospital for a while and then came home, but now he seemed weaker and more frail. They still shared their evenings together, but often her grandpa seemed too weak to make a fire after supper.

Then came the day when Marie got off the school bus to find her mother waiting for her. Taking Marie in her arms, she gently told her that Grandpa had died that day while sitting in his easy chair, smoking a pipe. It had been a painless, natural death, but for Marie it was the end of her young world.

Though she wore a brave face through the funeral and even the burial at the small country cemetery just down the road, inside she was inconsolable. Once more the storms of life raged and thundered in the young girl.

Still, life has a way of going on, and Marie and her mother survived. Now, every Saturday morning, the pair would walk down to the cemetery and visit Grandpa's grave beneath the weathered old oaks that lined the cemetery. Sometimes she would pick wildflowers from the roadside and lay them there as a present for her grandpa.

Since school was still in session, now Marie needed a baby sitter after school till her mother returned, but she vowed that no baby sitter other than Grandpa would do. Still, her mother arranged for a girl from town to drive out every day after she finished school to be with Marie until her mother returned from work. Since the high school got out later than Marie's elementary school, she would have to be alone for an hour before the babysitter arrived, but at age ten her mother judged that she was old enough to fend for herself for that short time.

Eventually, against her own prediction, Marie found that she liked her new baby sitter, who was reliable and kind. While she still missed her grandpa terribly, she started looking forward to time with her baby sitter, who could help Marie with her homework and knew fun games.

One day early in the spring of that year, as Marie got off the bus in front of her house, she heard an ominous sound behind her. Turning, she saw dark clouds hurrying their way in from the west, and in the distance she heard another deep rumble of thunder.

Fear brewing in her heart, she quickly flew to the house and locked herself in, praying that her baby sitter would get there before the storm hit. She didn't. An hour passed, and no baby sitter arrived. After an hour and a half, still alone, Marie heard the storm break in all its fury around the house. The wind whipped through the oak trees, and lightning flashed close by. Thunder exploded around her followed by the crash of a tree coming down in the distance. Marie sat huddled in the corner of the living room, hot tears coursing down her cheeks.

Panic broke over the girl. Running to the kitchen, she picked up the phone to call her mother, but the line was dead. Now shaking with fear and desperation, she replaced the phone on its cradle, silently praying that someone would come for her. In her panicked state, she began to wonder if she should go out into the storm and run through the rain and wind to a distant neighbor's house for safety.

As her tears turned to sobs, suddenly she was jolted back to reality by a single ring of the phone. Marie snatched for the phone like a drowning man grasps for a rope, but there was silence on the other end for a long moment. She was about to replace the receiver when to her bewilderment she heard a quiet voice. It was hazy and indistinct, as though from a long distance away, but the recognition of that voice stilled the beating of her heart at least for a moment. "It's OK, honey," came a gentle murmur, "you're safe. The storm will pass, and I'm right here. You don't think I would ever let anything happen to you, do you?" Then there was silence on the line once more.

Twenty minutes later, as the storm began to abate, Marie heard the roar of a car in the driveway quickly followed by a slamming door. Her mother burst into the house, her face clouded by fear. She found Marie sitting calmly on the couch, wearing a peaceful, almost serene, smile.

Her mother explained that she had received a phone call at work from the baby sitter; the girl had tried to get to the house, but the storm had torn through Oldenburg, uprooting trees and leaving power lines on the ground. Police had forbidden anyone from driving out of concern for public safety. Marie's mother explained that she had tried to call her, but the phone lines were dead, and so, in desperation, she had ignored the police warning and driven home. It had taken much longer than usual because she had to stop often to remove limbs from the road.

In a calm voice, Marie told her that she had received just one call—from her grandpa. At this news her mother's eyes snapped open wide, and she seemed about to say something, but then her nostrils flared for just a moment, and a look of bewildered recognition crossed her face. Marie understood—she had smelled it, too, ever since the phone rang. It was the rich, aromatic, delicious smell of pipe tobacco. Marie's mother said nothing, held her daughter close, and then without further discussion, made her a snack and put her to bed.

The next morning, Saturday, dawned bright and clear. Marie's mother suggested that the pair walk down the road to Grandpa's house, which was now vacant, to see if the storm had done any damage. Along the way, they could visit Grandpa's grave. As they walked through the beautiful morning, they made a game of tracing the telephone lines from pole to pole to see if they could find where the break had occurred the night before that had shut down their telephone service.

As Marie now recounts, the telephone line was intact until they reached the gate of the cemetery, where it suddenly went slack. Going inside, they found that a limb on the far side of the cemetery had severed the line completely, and the line had fallen onto the ground where the bare end rested…on her grandpa's grave.

Today Marie is of late middle age, and with a mixture of wisdom and nostalgia she goes on say that she has had some difficult times in her life since that day. She, like we all, has faced the storms of life. Yet, time and again, when things seemed most difficult, she says that she has heard in her mind a gentle, reassuring, and familiar voice—"It's OK, honey, you're safe. The storm will pass, and I'm right here. You don't think I would ever let anything happen to you, do you?"

A single tear welling up in her eye, she goes on to say that it is exactly at those moments that she has caught a whiff of the rich, aromatic, delicious scent of pipe tobacco.

Such is the story that Marie keeps close to her heart. Perhaps it is not a ghost story at all. Perhaps it's a story about family and about love. In the end, maybe it doesn't even matter. But this much is true—love is a powerful thing, and it would not be the first time that love had overcome the bounds of life and death itself.

2
THE GHOSTS OF STORY

When the words "ghost town" are uttered, images of the Old West immediately come to mind. A dusty, uninhabited main street with tumbleweeds blowing past the swinging doors of a long abandoned saloon is part and parcel of the common image of a ghost town. However, such towns are by no means the sole property of the Old West. Indeed, Indiana can boast of one striking example of a classic midwestern ghost town, now carefully and lovingly restored as a fascinating piece of Hoosier history. Further, if the stories told in and around this unique place are to be believed, then perhaps Story, Indiana truly is a ghost town in more than one sense of the word, for this is a town that is said to come with more than one ghost.

The history of Story, Indiana began in 1851 when Dr. George Story came to the area of Nashville, Indiana from southern Ohio. Story, a medical doctor, secured a land grant from President Millard Fillmore and began building the first structure of what was soon a thriving town. Throughout the next decades, the fortunes of the rural settlement, by now named after its founder, blossomed, and Story, Indiana became the largest and busiest settlement in the area. By the turn of the century, Story could boast two general stores, one church, a one-room schoolhouse, a grain mill, a sawmill, a slaughterhouse, a blacksmith's forge, and a post office. The town was a center of commerce and social activity for local farming families. For a time, it seemed that Story was fated to eclipse the nearby town of Nashville, which was then little more than a sleepy settlement.

In 1916, fire consumed the original structure in Story, the general store. However, even such a tragedy could not suppress the burgeoning hopes of the proprietors. The building was rebuilt on the original Civil War Era foundation and expanded to include a second story.

Sadly, this bright future would never be. The Great Depression, which cast its dark pall across the entire nation, ending the hopes and dreams of millions of Americans, also ended the hopes and dreams of Story. Between 1929 and 1933, nearly one-third of the residents of rural Indiana migrated from the area, most moving north toward Chicago or other urban centers in search of a better life. This emigration was particularly acute in Brown County, which lost about half of its population.

As farmers and patrons of Story businesses disappeared, one by one the shops along the main street were shuttered and abandoned. Time passed by Story, leaving it deserted and neglected. The once prosperous town seemed doomed to be a forgotten part of Indiana history.

Throughout most of the twentieth century, only the general store remained, eking out a meager trade in groceries and general merchandise. For a period of time, the upstairs portion of the building was utilized as a Studebaker buggy factory. However, with the advent of the automobile, even this source of revenue evaporated.

As is pointed out in the official history of Story (available via the Internet at www.storyinn.com), in retrospect, the lack of development in the next few years became a blessing for the town. While the majority of small towns throughout the state were swept up in the onrush of modernization, thus losing both their ambiance and charm, Story remained principally deserted and unchanged, seemingly frozen in time. Perversely, it is the very economic depravation that doomed the development of Story that is to thank for the fact that today, Story is arguably the best preserved settlement community in the Midwest.

The Story general store continued its meager trade until 1968 when its long time proprietor, Clothia Hedrick, sold it to two young people, a woman named Cynthia Shultz and a young man who went only by the name Benjamin. The pair did some renovation to the venerable old structure and turned the first floor into a restaurant that opened for business in 1970. Within the next several years, they continued to restore the building and eventually opened several rooms on the second floor as guest rooms for a bed and breakfast. The Story Inn was born and with it the impetus of new life to the community of Story.

From 1968 till 1994, the pair worked tirelessly on the project of restoring the surrounding community. Slowly, they began to acquire the surrounding parcels of land in the town until the entire town and all of its structures were theirs. Each building, in turn, was then renovated and turned into units for the inn.

In 1994, the enterprising pair sold the business and the land they had acquired to a developer who ran the inn until 1998. However, the business did not generate the income necessary to keep it financially afloat.

It was then that Indianapolis attorney Richard Hofstetter and his partner Frank Mueoler became interested in the Story Inn. The pair had worked together on the development of a historic parcel in Indianapolis and both were intrigued to learn about the community of Story. "I have a soft spot in my heart for old buildings and old places," Hofstetter says. "We found out about this place, and I knew that the bank was going to take it and carve it out into parcels. Frank and I wanted to preserve its integrity as a town and that's what we set out to do."

Purchasing all twenty-three acres of the property, the pair set to work, further renovating the inn and restaurant as well as the nine main buildings in the town. Today Story stands meticulously and lovingly restored to its original condition. To walk down its main street is to journey back in history to a simpler, more rustic time.

The town itself looks precisely as it did in the last days of the nineteenth century. Virtually every structure in the town, from the gristmill to Dr. Story's home itself, has been converted for use as guest cottages for the inn. Wood sided buildings support classic tin roofs. Inside, visitors find hardwood floors beneath stamped tin ceilings, antique furniture, and a décor that fits the nineteenth century surroundings. Indeed, much care has been given to preserve the ambiance of the buildings despite the introduction of such modern amenities as hot tubs and kitchenettes.

The former general store, the only structure in Story to continually function as a commercial enterprise, remains the centerpiece of the town. At first glance, the building still strongly resembles the frontier general store it was for so many decades. Outside, two antique gas pumps stand guard, a reminder of the time when quick marts and modern service stations were not yet imagined. Entering the building, one is immediately drawn to a functioning potbellied stove, which sends its warm glow throughout the room.

The main floor has been converted for use as a fine dining restaurant. Where once dry goods and farm implements were sold, now waiters wind their way bearing bottles of fine wine and gourmet entrées. The walls are decorated with pictures of the area and examples of the goods once sold at the store. Overall, the restaurant pervades an atmosphere of rustic charm and genteel elegance.

Upstairs, the second floor of the inn has been transformed into guest rooms. All, save one, bear the name of a person famous in the history of the town or region. One room, however, is named for a figure more legendary than any in local history. Hers is a name steeped in lore and mystery and one that has led many to question if perhaps the antique town of Story might be a true "ghost town" in more than one sense of the term. She is the celebrated Blue Lady of the Story Inn.

Though reported encounters with this enigmatic feminine phantom go back many years, Richard Hofstetter's familiarity with her goes back to 1995, shortly after he and his partner had embarked on their venture in Story. "When I came here, I had no idea about anything regarding a ghost," he now recalls, "but shortly after we started renovating the general store, we went up into the attic and found a treasure trove of old materials relating to the inn and general store. In the pile were old journals that had been kept in the rooms for people to write in after they had stayed overnight. Once I got around to reading them, I was startled to find that there were literally dozens of references to people encountering strange things, particularly in this one room."

While the experiences reputed in the journals did vary, more than once visitors recorded glimpsing the wispy apparition of a woman in white in and around what is now the Blue Lady Room. "She never had a name," Hofstetter says, "but when we were going through the attic, we found an old print of a woman standing in the moonlight—her skin is kind of blue and she is wearing long flowing white robes. She reminded us of the woman they had described, so we started calling her 'The Blue Lady,' and it stuck."

Whatever name given her, it readily becomes apparent that whoever, or whatever, the Blue Lady might be, she is certainly an active, if benign, presence in the inn.

It is through reading the journals placed in the rooms (a practice that continues to this day) that much of her activity can be ascertained. Journal entries purporting to relate encounters with the specter vary from the simply odd to some that defy explanation. Perhaps one of the more direct episodes was documented by a female guest some years ago. According to the journal entry she left behind:

> Although the day had begun quite sensibly, we knew by 10:38 P.M. that we had entered another dimension. After a swell meal downstairs...we retired to the room to recall our youth. We had coddled and prepared all the parts of our bodies which, at our ages, require attention each and every night and... turned out the blue light and snuggled under the covers...Just as Carl was making advances, a blue shadow crossed the bed. Our heads whipped around and any thoughts of romance folded. The ghost—after glancing at herself in the large mirror—arranged her skirts and plopped on the shelf and dresser and looked us square in the face. Carl pulled the blanket up to his eyes and I sat bolt upright. The ghost began to whistle and fix her nails. After some minutes, she floated to my side of the bed (the window side) and pinched my bottom (which was still

> encased in a black lace thing I had bought…for this special night, our anniversary). Startled by this display of familiarity from a ghost I had only just seen nine minutes before, I leaped from the bed, ran to the bathroom and into the little toilet closet. No sooner had I turned around than the door slammed back…I heard the ghost give a slight whoosh…[In the morning] there, on my side of the bed, was a blue hair ribbon and a false fingernail.

Despite the somewhat tongue-in-cheek tone of this entry, it is by no means the only encounter with the Blue Lady recorded in the journals. Another couple who stayed in the room in April of 1997 related the following encounter:

> I met the "Blue Lady" of Story, IN. It was Saturday night at 10:10 P.M. and I was sitting in the corner rocking chair gazing out the back door. I kept feeling like somebody was watching me. The next thing I knew I was staring at the face of the "Blue Lady" in the glass of the back door. Her deep piercing blue eyes were hypnotic and I felt as if I could not look away…

photo courtesy of Abigail Wilkins

Exterior of the Story Inn, Story, Indiana

Still another couple to stay in the room several years ago related their nocturnal encounter with the illusive phantom:

> Last night I did feel that someone was in the room with me, but when I turned around, no one was there. Yet I did not imagine this. I don't believe in ghosts. I also saw my husband bolt from a deep sleep at 1:00 A.M. and look at the window and vividly describe a woman in a blue dress that was there. He then quickly fell back asleep. This morning I asked him about it and he had no recollection. Too weird!

According to the reports described in the guest books, at moments, the Blue Lady is more felt than actually seen. One such report came from a couple who occupied the room two days before Halloween of 2000:

> Last night was the only time we have experienced another presence in the room besides our own. I was sitting at the dresser when I noticed the scent of perfume. I thought it might be my own, but it got much stronger. It was then that I realized it was the scent of roses that I was smelling. I dismissed the rose scent as someone's room freshener and we locked up and went to dinner. When we got back upstairs to rest for a while before taking a carriage ride, my husband went to wash his hands while I sat down to read. He came back complaining that I had turned the air conditioning on, which I had not. He said that it felt like something cold had brushed up against him and gave him the goosebumps. I was getting a little nervous but did not want to alarm him. The last thing that happened on our stay was in the middle of the night when I was awakened by a breath on my face. It smelled of roses. After that it was pretty hard to sleep. It could have been my imagination playing with my head—I guess we will find out next time we come to visit.

Other visitors have left accounts of doors opening and closing by themselves, objects being moved from obvious locations only to be replaced in their original locations, and lights that have turned off and on apparently of their own volition.

Room guests are not the only ones who have encountered inexplicable phenomena in the building. Staff members have also reported repeated encounters that have led them to question if perhaps a more permanent guest has taken up residence at the inn.

Tonya Bokich, an employee, reports a strange incident that occurred on October 31 (an apropos day for such happenings) of 2001. The tale centers around the poster of the Blue Lady that had been found in the attic and placed in a frame to hang on the wall of the Blue Lady Room.

On the day in question, Ms. Bokich was busy preparing the guest rooms on the second floor for guests who would be arriving that night. "After we clean, we always leave the doors open upstairs for people to take a quick peek if they just come by," she now says. "The rooms were already cleaned, and we had done a walk through to inspect them. I remember that there was nobody staying upstairs at that moment—they were all going to be arriving that night. I don't even think that there was anyone in the office that day."

"Anyway," she continues, "late that afternoon I did a second walk-through of the second floor, and there, lying on the floor in the Blue Lady Room, was this poster of the Blue Lady. It had come off the wall and flown at least six feet across the room to land where I found it. It must have fallen with some considerable force, too, because the glass was broken and we had to buy a new frame for it."

Ms. Bokich also echoes an experience mentioned more than once in the guest journals—a propensity for one door in the room to open by itself. "There is a door in the room that leads out to overlook the garden," Ms. Bokich explains, "and it has a sliding lock on it. You have to slide it all the way over to unlock it, and it is not all that easy. Anyway, it is not that uncommon that we will clean a room after a guest has left, locking the door only to come back later and find the lock undone and the door standing open. This has happened several times in one day. It's strange to say the least."

Tonya has also had strange experiences with another door on the upper floor of the inn. What makes these experiences doubly strange is the fact that the door in question is not one readily accessible to workers.

"In one of the rooms upstairs, we have an overhead attic door. It is maybe six or seven feet off the floor. You can't reach it without using a broom or maybe standing on a ladder, and there is a slide lock on it. Last year, there were several times inside a two-month period that we would find it standing wide open. We would do a walk-through and everything would be shut up, and then I would come through just a little while later only to find it standing wide open. I had to get a broom to shut it."

These strange antics regarding the doors have even extended to the basement of the inn, which has been the site of several unusual occurrences. "One time a couple of the workers went downstairs," Ms. Bokich remembers. "In the middle of the evening they had heard a crash from the basement. When they went down, they found the door to the basement completely off of its hinges. It is a solid door that is pretty heavy, and it had been lifted right off of its hinges. There was no one in the basement at the time, and there was no way that it could have happened by accident."

Tonya also describes similar experiences with lamps, not only in the Blue Lady Room, but throughout the second floor. "We've had reports all throughout the second floor of lights turning on and off by themselves," she says. "The lights have been weird. I come up to double check the rooms before people check in, and I turn on the lights, of course, and then I would walk through again in a few minutes, and the lights would be off. So, I would turn them back on. This happened several times. These were lamps, not wall switches. I just say, 'OK, Blue Lady, you don't like that light on, but we have to have it on for the guests.' I talk to her if stuff is going on, and that seems to slow things down a bit."

Others who have worked in and around the inn have reported similar experiences. One particularly chilling event occurred several years ago when several workers were cleaning up the kitchen area after the dining room had closed for the evening. As Richard Hofstetter tells the tale, while the workers pursued their cleaning duties, one produced a small rubber ball, which they proceeded to bounce on the floor as they worked. At one point the ball, taking an errant bounce, rolled out of the kitchen and down the stairs toward the basement. As one of the workers turned to descend the stairs to retrieve the ball, his progress was arrested by a singular rhythmic thumping coming toward them from the basement area. As the workers watched, transfixed, an unbelievable sight met their eyes. Against all logic and the laws of physics, the ball came bounding toward them up the stairs. Slowly, the ball emerged from the darkness of the basement stairwell and rolled to a stop at the feet of one of the workers. Needless to say, the workers quickly finished their tasks and left the building in some haste.

While the Blue Lady Room seems to be a center of inexplicable phenomena at the inn, many such events have also been reported from the dining room and kitchen. Many years ago, several workers and patrons witnessed the sight of a votive candle sitting on top of an antique iron stove in the entryway of the dining room slide across the length of the stove, apparently under its own power, and crash to the floor.

Mr. Hofstetter also recalls a bizarre incident that related to a picture that hangs along one wall in the dining room. "It is an antique photograph of an old lady that was hanging on the wall when we got here. We had the picture propped up against the back of the rolltop desk in the area of the store that served as the old post office," Richard remembers. "On the night in question, it was a busy Sunday, and the dining room was filled with people. I was watching the desk and answering the phone, and several waiters were running around doing their jobs. One of them, Seth Gilbert, was a man in his early twenties who had been working as a waiter for us for a while."

"We were both taking a breather," Mr. Hofstetter continues, "and I was having a Coke. Seth and I were standing looking at this picture, and I made the comment, 'She wasn't real pretty in her day,' and he laughed. Immediately, as the words left my mouth, the picture pitched suddenly and violently forward off the desk, as though it had been brushed off by a hand. We both saw it happen. It really freaked us out. The first words out of Seth's mouth were, 'I'm so sorry!' And then we both just blew up laughing. Now, that is not anything that I can explain."

It should be noted that the spirit of the Blue Lady, if she indeed haunts the Story Inn, is a benign presence, content to express herself in a manner more mischievous than truly frightening. Indeed, on at least some occasions she is said to have been helpful. One waitress tells the story of opening the inn one frosty winter morning only to find, upon entering, fresh coffee brewing in the pot. Subsequent investigation revealed that the coffee was fresh despite the fact that she was the first one in the building that day.

Another waitress tells of coming to work early one morning in December of 2001 to find the heat in the inn turned on and the dining room warm and welcoming. What made this event strange was the fact that there was no timer on the furnace, and since she had been the last one out the previous night, she knew she had turned the furnace down to its lowest setting. Perhaps it was the Blue Lady, graciously welcoming the workers to what is still her home.

Other workers have noticed odd events. Douglas Adams has worked in the inn since it was purchased, first as a waiter in the dining room and then as a bookkeeper. During his time there, he has experienced several strange episodes throughout the facility. One transpired in November of 2001 when he was working late in the office.

"We were in the office—Rick, Frank, myself, and the General Manger at the time," Mr. Adams recalls. "Everybody else had gone home for the night. These guys went to the bar and David went home, and I was in the office putting stuff away when I heard someone coming up the stairs. I thought one of these guys was standing behind me, and I turned around to say 'What?' and there was nobody standing there. The odd thing was that I felt like there was somebody else in the room, and I felt this odd pricking sensation across my face—like someone was touching my cheeks. At that point I felt complete panic, and I felt this emotion of 'LEAVE.' That is exactly what I did."

Mr. Adams has also been witness to several seemingly inexplicable incidents in the first floor dining room section of the inn. "One of the things that happens with some regularity is glasses suddenly breaking at the tables," he says. This may sound normal for a dining room, but in these cases the patrons swear they were not touching the glasses at the time. Customers will say, 'It just broke—we didn't ever touch it!' and by now we believe them."

Mr. Adams also reports strange phenomena in the historic old building. "You think you see things in your peripheral vision, and then there is the sound of voices. You can hear people talking all the time," Mr. Adams continues, warming to the subject. "You think someone is around. You hear murmuring; you hear people walking around—particularly in the kitchen. You think, 'Oh, there's someone back there,' and when you go back there, no one is there."

Despite these strange and seemingly unsettling events, Mr. Adams, like all of the workers at the inn, does not feel in the least way threatened by them. "I feel very, very safe here," he says. "I am here every night—I am the last one out; I shut off the lights and lock up the doors, and I have never felt scared. This is a safe place. Just whistle and it will go away."

Indeed, despite the eerie goings-on that seem to happen with regularity at the Story Inn, the structure pervades an atmosphere of warmth and hospitality. Workers and guests alike cannot escape the charm that permeates the grounds of the inn. Still, in the midst of this beautifully rustic setting, the strange incidents continue.

If, as suggested by some, there is a spectral presence of the "Blue Lady" at the Story Inn, then she seems to have ghostly company on

photo courtesy of Abigail Wilkins

Exterior of the Doc Story House in Story, Indiana

the grounds. A short distance away from the inn, the Doc Story Home boasts its own collection of unearthly tales. This home, which was one of the original buildings on the site, served as the private home of Dr. Story, and today has been renovated into an elegant and inviting guest house. Perhaps it is the very historical ambiance of the building that has, as some believe, contributed to the continued presence of at least one spirit who may have overstayed his earthly welcome.

Like the Blue Lady of the Story Inn, this is a specter who is content to merely make himself known in gentle ways and who, at worst, is capable of displaying a mischievous and slightly bawdy temperament.

Such was the experience of one female worker who regularly cleans the Doc Story House between guests. She reports that on more than one occasion, while bending over to vacuum the home, she has distinctly felt the sensation of being pinched by an unseen, but certainly felt, presence. Other times, she says that she has heard her name called while in the home, only to search the premises to find that she was alone.

This worker is by no means alone in her conviction that something unnatural is present in the home. Visitors have frequently reported the smell of cherry pipe tobacco in the upper section of the house. Others have heard people talking on the front porch late at night when the porch itself is devoid of human occupants. Journal entries left in the Doc Story House reveal tales of phantom footsteps climbing the stairs and sights and sounds that seem to be echoes of a far distant time.

While such tales may, upon first hearing, sound bizarre and somewhat dubious to those unacquainted with the town of Story, if heard within the context of the rustic ambiance of the property itself, they seem almost natural. It may be the very idyllic air of the property that lends itself so well to tales of visitors from another time.

Of course, the questions remain. Does the spirit of the beautiful Blue Lady truly walk the oaken floors of the Story Inn? Does Doctor Story himself still reside in the home he loved and the town he spent so much of his life developing? In the end, the truth will remain delightfully unknown and unknowable. As owner Richard Hofstetter states in his review of the ghostly tales, "Personally, I still do not believe in the

Blue Lady, though I may change my mind if I someday see her for myself. However, I am convinced that this is not your typical urban legend. There are too many first hand reports from credible people. As a lawyer, I have won cases on evidence that was less compelling."

Perhaps the questions regarding the spirits of Story should remain in the realm of the mysterious. Some things are better left to the wonder and mystery of life. If, as the tales suggest, spirits still roam the rustic and beautiful setting, they could ask for no better locale for their haunts. They are as much a part of our shared history as the town itself, which may truly lay claim to being Indiana's only authentic "ghost town."

Perhaps the best homage to this legendary lady comes from an ode written for her by the local musical group Slats Klug and the Liar's Bench, appropriately entitled "Blue Lady Blue."

> I saw you, Blue Lady, when I turned on your light
> Felt a breeze on my neck, smelled cherry smoke of your pipe
> Does this cold holiday bring a blue memory?
> Have you something to say? Will you say it to me?
> I've heard that December's when you haunt these old halls.
> Is it then you remember? Is it a lover who calls?
> At the inn out at Story your story's made fame
> Flicker the candle...whisper your name.
> Blue Lady Blue, what happened to you?
> ...Tell me, tell me true
> What can I do, just for you?
> Oh tell me why...why so blue, Lady Blue?
> Your room by the garden has a sapphire glow
> Begging your pardon, have you nowhere to go?
> Some they do quiver when the house grows late
> But I pray for the shiver and I wait and I wait.
> Blue Lady Blue, what happened to you?
> ...Tell me, tell me true
> What can I do, just for you?
> Oh tell me why...why so blue, Lady Blue.

3
THE HOUSE CALL

Some ghost stories are public in nature. From their nebulous beginnings, they attract immediate attention and rapidly work their way into the lore of a community. Such stories quickly weave themselves into the very fabric of our common consciousness, and the "fame" of the specters in question is assured.

Other tales are of a more private nature. Far from the average myth of public consumption, such tales are held within closed groups such as families, often for generations. In some cases the chilling tales are handed down from generation to generation, like macabre family heirlooms, protected and even cherished.

Here is one story handed down for many years within a respected family of La Porte, Indiana. Told from father to child to grandchild, perhaps expanded with each retelling, it has been part of the private lore of this venerable family until its presentation today by Elizabeth Palmer.

Ms. Palmer, a middle-aged accounting executive, sits back in her chair as she begins to reveal a story that is indeed a cherished family heirloom. While some might regard the account as nothing more than an odd family narrative, it readily becomes apparent as she warms to her tale that it is a story bearing much significance for her.

As Ms. Palmer describes the story, in the fall of 1921, her great-grandfather, Dr. Uriah Scott,* moved to La Porte to begin his medical practice. Just a few years after his service in World War I and fresh from medical school, Dr. Scott was anxious to begin his career and new life. La Porte, a growing city, seemed an ideal place to do both, and his practice quickly flourished. Two years later, Dr. Scott married Mildred Lake, a daughter of one of the leading families in the area, and the two settled into a fine new home near downtown.

As Dr. Scott later told the tale to his children (and they to their children), one evening early in November of his first year of marriage, he and his new wife were at home enjoying a warm fire on a cold night. Suddenly, their bliss was disturbed by an incessant rapping on their door. Although he had been in medical practice a few short years, Dr. Scott had already become accustomed to late-night visitors requesting emergency house calls. However, on this night, with a cold wind whistling outside, it was with some reluctance that he tore himself away from the warmth of the fire and the beauty of his new wife to answer the call.

As he opened the door, a cold breath of wind rushed past, but the brief chill that coursed through him went beyond the icy bite of the night. Standing before him was an imposing figure. He was tall and thin, and held himself very erect, with a regal air. Dr. Scott judged the man to be of late middle age, with gray hair and eyebrows over two of the most piercing eyes he had ever seen. Curiously, Dr. Scott noted that he wore an old fashioned greatcoat, opened to reveal a long-outdated formal suit.

"Are you the doctor?" asked the stranger in a tone that was formal without a pretense of cordiality.

"Yes," stammered back the physician, "I'm Dr. Scott. Is there something that..."

"My daughter," the stranger interrupted coldly, "she's been injured. You will please follow me to my home and tend to her." There was something in the stranger's tone that suggested a man who was used to having his orders followed immediately and without question.

Briefly glancing beyond the doorstep and into the night, Dr. Scott was surprised to see, standing in the yard beyond the mysterious stranger, an old-fashioned horse and buggy. In the early 1920s, automobiles were becoming a common sight in town, and horse-drawn buggies as a means of conveyance had been relegated to rural farmers. Still, there was nothing in the image and bearing of this man to suggest a rural farmer. Another jolt of uneasiness crept though the young doctor, yet the oath of his profession dictated that he must respond. "Yes, all right, let me get my coat and I'll follow you," he murmured.

Turning back to the firelight, Dr. Scott reached for his coat and then, on impulse, asked his wife if she would like to join him on his call. Somehow her company might ease the disquiet he felt about this particular summons. She agreed, and the two ventured out to their Model T Ford parked next to the house. Slowly, the pair followed the horse and buggy through downtown La Porte and deep into the countryside. After traveling for some time, they turned up yet another country lane Dr. Scott had never noticed before. Again, they traveled for long minutes through the darkness and wind without any destination in sight. Indeed, Dr. Scott had begun to wonder if he were the victim of some bizarre prank or wild-goose chase when the clouds, driven by the wild night wind, parted and the full moon shone down on a strange sight.

It was a mansion, at least by northern Indiana standards. Three stories high, it stood imperially, with a wide veranda on which stood tall columns. Dr. Scott thought it odd that he had never heard talk in town of this imposing structure, which looked like it would have been more at home in the New England countryside or the antebellum south.

Slowly, the horse and buggy leading them stopped, and Dr. Scott could see the stranger dismount and go to the door of the house. Turning to his wife, Dr. Scott heard himself unconsciously speaking in a whisper. "Why don't you stay right here?" he said. "It's probably not much—just a routine case, and I'll be right back."

Dr. Scott had reason to doubt this assumption as he noticed what appeared to be fresh blood painting the threshold. More blood seemed to be dotted along the wall of the hallway, yet the stranger made no explanation as he wordlessly led Dr. Scott up a tall stairway to the second floor. Following his mysterious host through another door, Dr. Scott found himself in a small bedroom. Huddled on the bed lay a girl of about seventeen, her shoulder wrapped in a sheet. Fresh blood was freely seeping though the cloth. Feigning professional courtesy, Dr. Scott went to the girl and, bending close, gently asked her name. In place of a reply, she looked away.

Now Dr. Scott's professional instincts took over, and without formalities he unwound the sheet to find what appeared to be a fresh gunshot wound. He could clearly trace the trajectory of the bullet as it grazed the shoulder muscle and passed out though the girl. The wound itself was not life threatening, yet the sight of a gunshot wound on a young woman brought back the sense of foreboding he had been fighting since the first knock at his door that evening. Now rattled, Dr. Scott turned to the strange man who stood looking on intently from the doorway. "What happened here?" he asked incredulously, "This girl's been shot!"

"An accident," the man replied almost contemptuously. "I was cleaning a hunting rifle and it went off. Her wounds are not life threatening, I think." His voice, unnaturally cold, cut through the air like a knife.

Returning to his silent patient, Dr. Scott opened his Gladstone bag and gathered what he would need to treat the wound. He then cleaned, dressed, and bandaged the gash. While he did so, his patient lay silently on the bed, except for an occasional whimper. His task finished, Dr. Scott again turned to the girl's father. "This will do for tonight, but you had better bring her into my office tomorrow. This bandage will need to be changed, and we don't want infection to set in." At these words, Dr. Scott saw something quickly pass through the face of his host. It seemed a strange mixture of rage and sadness, yet it was quickly replaced with the steely face he had maintained throughout the procedure.

After a moment, he nodded and Dr. Scott began to repack his bag. However, as he turned to go, he glanced once more at his young patient lying prone on the bed before him. Their eyes locked, and he froze. As he would later describe, in her eyes he saw a desperation and hopelessness that was both pathetic and frightening. It was as though she was silently begging him to take her away with him. In a second, however, he heard the man behind him clearing his throat and then speaking in his clipped, icy tones. "She will be fine now, Doctor. You have done your job, and we must not keep your wife waiting any longer than necessary. Thank you."

Sensing a dismissal, Dr. Scott reluctantly took his leave of the home and returned to his car. Climbing back in, he began to tell his wife about the strange visit but stopped short at the sight of his wife huddled against the far door, shaking with fear. "What's wrong?" inquired Dr. Scott.

"Don't leave just yet," came her reply. "I think there's a man injured over there—behind that woodpile." Pointing at a pile of brush and fallen limbs a few yards away, she continued. "Shortly after you went into the house, I began to hear a moaning from that direction. It was terrible—like someone in great pain. Then, when the moon came out, I thought I saw a man struggling to get up and then falling back again. You have to go to him!" she concluded earnestly.

Again clutching his bag, Dr. Scott ventured out into the darkness, every sense on edge from the events of the night. In a few moments, however, he returned to the car, relieved. Climbing inside, he tried to comfort his still frightened wife. "There was nothing behind that pile of wood," he said trying to sound cheerful. "It was probably just a wild animal you heard, and the moonlight can play strange tricks on the eyes. Don't worry; everything will be all right. Tomorrow the father will bring that girl in, and we will get everything straightened out." Starting the car, the pair began their slow journey toward the sanity of their home.

The next day, as Dr. Scott went through his routine of office patients, he kept a wary eye out for the girl and her father, yet they never appeared. When a second day passed and he had still not seen them, he knew what he must do. That afternoon, when his office hours ended, he walked the short distance to the County Courthouse and made his way to the sheriff's office. There he told the deputy on duty that he wished to make a report of a visit he had made a few nights earlier.

As fate would have it, the deputy on duty that day was an officer who was just a few years short of retirement, having served his community for over thirty years. A genial, friendly man, he asked Dr. Scott back to the office, offered him a cup of coffee, and taking out a pen and pad, asked him what had occurred. His bemused expression told Dr. Scott that he was expecting nothing more than a routine report.

As Dr. Scott began to tell his story, however, he noticed that the deputy's face began to cloud. He had just begun to describe the house to which he had been taken when the deputy put down his pen and looked very directly at Dr. Scott. In an official tone that was much different from the greeting he had given just a few minutes before, the deputy said, "There is no need for you to finish the story, Doctor, and I can promise that you won't see that girl or her father again."

Taken aback, Dr. Scott asked, "What makes you say that, Deputy? How can you be so sure?"

The deputy stared at the floor for a while as though lost in thought, and then looked back to the young physician. "Maybe it would be better if you came with me. There is something I think you need to see."

Perplexed, Dr. Scott agreed, and they walked out through the courthouse to the deputy's car. Together they drove in silence through downtown and out into the country. With a rising sense of discomfort, Dr. Scott realized that, while he had not described the route he had driven two nights before, they were nevertheless following it exactly. As the buildings of downtown receded into the distance, the deputy broke the awkward silence as, without introduction, he began his story.

"Many years ago, just after the Civil War, a rich businessman moved from out east to the outskirts of La Porte. They say that he had bought a timber business in Indiana, and I guess he wanted to be closer to the operation. He built a mansion just east of town for himself and his daughter. I never heard what had happened to the mother, but I do know the girl was his only family in the world. The old-timers say he was fiercely protective of the girl, to the point that he controlled her every move.

"By the time she was sixteen," he continued, "she had grown into a beautiful young thing. A lot of the local boys came to call, but her father drove them off. He said that when it was time for her to marry he would take her back east and find her a husband from one of the proper families of New England. He never got the chance."

According to the tale the deputy told, the girl had already secretly met and fallen in love with a boy from the area. "He was a no-account day laborer, but she loved him," he added. "When the old man discovered their relationship, he forbade them to ever see each other again. Then, one night he came home unexpectedly from a business trip and found her in the boy's arms in the hallway."

His voice grew graver yet as he went on, "They say the old man flew into a rage. From underneath his greatcoat, he drew a pistol and shot at the boy, but the girl leapt in front of her lover. The bullet grazed her shoulder, and she fell into a heap at the boy's feet." According to the deputy's tale, on instinct the boy bent toward her prone form, but as he did, the father shot again, striking the young man squarely in the chest.

"He dragged the boy out into the yard behind a woodpile to die," the deputy continued, "and took his daughter upstairs and bandaged her wound, which did not seem too bad. He didn't dare to call a doctor for fear that his crime would be discovered. He tended her the best he could, but infection set in, and a week or so later she died."

Again, for a long moment, silence filled the car, and then the deputy concluded his story. "From what I understand, after the girl's death, the old man lost all interest in everything, even his business. A couple of years later, they say he sat down at his desk, wrote out a full confession of what he had done, and then went to the attic and hanged himself."

Breaking from the spell of the story, Dr. Scott turned toward the deputy. "This has to be just a story—how could you possibly know all of this?" he asked incredulously.

"Because," came the policeman's slow, measured reply, "twenty-five years ago I was locking up the courthouse one night when I was stopped by an old man in a black suit. He asked if there was a doctor in town, and when I said our only doctor was gone visiting relatives, he told me his daughter had been injured. He asked if I would go with him to help her. I went to the very same house you described and bandaged the same girl."

"I knew a gunshot wound when I saw one, and so I asked the old man to come to my office and make a report. When he didn't come in the next day, I drove back to the house, and what I saw there cost me many a night's sleep since then."

"What did you see?" asked Dr. Scott, unsure that he really wanted an answer.

"This," the deputy replied, and with that he pulled his car to a stop.

Before them spread the house, or what was left of it. The roof was caved in on one side, and the majestic porch lay in ruins. Remnants of the columns could be seen strewn about on the weed-covered yard. The house was as dead as those who had once lived in it.

After gazing at the scene for a long moment, Dr. Scott was numbly aware of the deputy speaking once again. "I have thought about it a lot," he whispered, "and I think it's the guilt that keeps him coming back. Not guilt about the boy—I don't think there was anything human enough in him to care about that. No, it's the guilt about his daughter—the guilt over killing the only thing he had ever loved that keeps him coming back, trying to get her the care in death that he denied her in life."

According to Dr. Scott's great-granddaughter, he returned to his home that afternoon and said nothing to his wife. Many years passed before he would relate to her all that had happened. However, he later said that more than a few times over the next several months he would awaken from a troubled sleep, almost sure that he had heard an insistent rapping on his front door. On the few occasions he ventured to that door and opened it, he was greeted only by the wind and the darkness.

Sometime in the 1940s, a fire swept away the remains of the old home, and today no one is sure where it once stood. However, in a curious footnote, Ms. Palmer fishes in her purse for a moment and then produces a newspaper clipping from the 1960s that her mother had preserved. The story in question concerns a new housing development that had been built on the east side of La Porte, and a curious series of pranks that had been perpetrated on the new residents there.

According to the report, those moving into the new homes had told police that they had been disturbed by someone apparently knocking on doors late at night, only to disappear. Numerous reports of this type had been lodged with the police. However, after investigating, police admitted they were baffled with regard to who would perpetrate such an annoyance. However, Elizabeth Palmer and the rest of the descendents of Uriah Scott believe that they know. They think it is the unquiet spirit of a father, seeking care for his injured daughter.

Of course, the entire tale might well be apocryphal, perhaps invented by Dr. Scott for the amusement of his children. But when the wind blows cold and clouds billow past a full moon east of La Porte, a dark figure might still roam, seeking aid and perhaps even redemption, beyond the boundaries of life and death and in the hazy realm of Indiana ghostlore.

4
THE RETURN OF THE BLACK WIDOW

It was in the predawn hours of a spring morning near a small town in northern Indiana that one of the most gruesome true stories of all time began to unfold. Before the months of prolonged horror were over, this town would receive a national, even international, reputation as the home of a Lady MacBeth, a moral monster, a fiend incarnate. It would be the scene of one of the most puzzling mysteries in the annals of crime. A newspaper of the day correctly predicted that what happened here would not be forgotten for a generation, and the people of La Porte, Indiana still remember.

—Sylvia Shepherd, "The Mistress Of Murder Hill"[1]

Such begins one of the strangest and most macabre chapters in Indiana history. It is a tale that dawns in a dark legacy of horror and murder unique in the annals of American crime and ends with a mystery that endures to this day.

The tale originated with a spark of fire. In the early morning hours of April 28, 1908, Joseph Maxson, a hired hand on a forty-eight-acre farm on McClung Road, just outside La Porte, woke in his upstairs room in the farmhouse from what seemed a bad dream. As he later reported to officials, he was roused from a deep sleep around 4:00 A.M. to find his room rapidly filling with smoke. Jumping from his bed, Maxson looked out the window to see the brick portion of the house engulfed in flames. He next ran down the inner stairs of the house to the door leading to that section of the home and pounded, calling for the other residents. Receiving no answer, he made an exit through a rear stairwell leading outside in order to save himself.

Revived by the fresh night air, Maxson went to the front entrance of the home in a valiant, yet futile, attempt to kick in the door. Finally, in desperation, the hired hand resorted to throwing a brick through a large window at the front of the house in an effort to gain entrance but was repulsed by the roaring flames.

His attempts were not without cause; he knew the house contained several people: Mrs. Belle Gunness, the homeowner, and her children.

By now the light from the flames had attracted the attention of a neighbor, Mr. William Clifford, and the two continued in their attempts to enter the home. Together they managed to break through a door pane only to be forced back when a streak of flame shot though the door and into the night. Now, aided by another neighbor, William Humphry, they placed a ladder against an upper floor window. Peering into an upstairs bedroom belonging to one of the children, Humphry saw nothing but an empty bed. They moved the ladder to the window of a second bedroom, and again, Humphry peered in only to find it, too, unoccupied. It was the first in what would be an increasing spiral of mysteries.

By now frustrated in their attempts at rescue, one of the men rode to town to summon help, and at about 5:00 A.M. Sheriff Albert Smutzer and Deputy Sheriff William Anstiss arrived with a contingent of the local fire department bearing hooks and ladders. At this point, however, nothing could be done since the house was totally engulfed. By 8:00 A.M., with a crowd of over fifty neighbors and townspeople watching, the flames had subsided enough that the firemen could begin the gruesome task of searching through the ruins for human remains.

At first, nothing was recovered except the scorched remnants of household articles such as bedding and clothing. Several hours later, the searchers were nearly ready to give up their quest when they reached the southeast corner of the home. Finally, removing charred timber and debris, a cavern was revealed leading to the basement area of the home. It was at that point that what seemed to be a routine fire investigation took a gruesome and ominous turn.

Within the scorched and still smoldering basement lay a mattress, upon which could be seen the charred remains of four corpses. Though nearly completely incinerated, it was obvious that three of the bodies were children, the smallest of which, a boy, was laying across the arm of an adult female body. As though this nightmarish scenario was not enough to cause even the most hardened rescue worker to recoil, what added an even greater degree of horror to the scene was the fact that the female body was apparently headless.

The location of the corpses in the basement of the home, as well as the apparent decapitation of the female, immediately gave rise to the suggestion of murder. Further evidence of foul play was indicated by the fact that the bodies were found beneath the remains of a piano, which had been housed on the first floor living room. This indicated that the bodies had been placed in the basement prior to the ignition of the fire.

With the charge of murder now hanging in the air, it did not take long for Sheriff Smutzer to name Ray Lamphere, a former hired hand at the farm, as his chief suspect. Lamphere had worked at the farm for more than a year before an apparent falling out with Mrs. Gunness some time previously. In the months before the mysterious fire, Mrs. Gunness had gone to the local police department several times reporting that Lamphere had been stalking her and had appeared numerous times at the farm making ominous threats against her and her family.

The fact that he had been charged twice (and convicted once) for trespassing on the Gunness' farm had apparently not dissuaded Lamphere's attentions. In fact, at one point Mrs. Gunness had attempted, unsuccessfully, to have him declared legally insane. All in all, it seemed like a sound circumstantial case could be made against Ray Lamphere with regard to the murder of Belle Gunness. Before the last embers of the fire at the farm were out, a manhunt had begun.

Later that day, Lamphere was found at a nearby farm and arrested. While he admitted to traveling through the vicinity of the farm that morning and even to seeing the fire from a distance, he steadfastly maintained his innocence regarding its origin.

By now, what had started as a routine fire investigation had turned into a murder inquiry into the death of Belle Gunness and her three children. In all probability, the story might have ended with the trial and possible execution of a disgruntled hired hand, except for the fact that for all the players in this drama, and for the town of La Porte itself, the story was about to take an unimaginable turn.

This portion of the drama began inconspicuously enough with the arrival of Asle Helgelein, a Norwegian farmer from Mansfield, South Dakota, on May 1. Mr. Helgelein came to La Porte in search of news regarding his brother, Andrew. Andrew Helgelein, a farmer from Aberdeen, had left his home on January 2 of that year, telling his family only that he would be gone about a week. When he did not return as expected, Asle went to Aberdeen to search through his brother's belongings for some hint as to his whereabouts. Among his personal effects, Asle was surprised to find several letters from Belle Gunness, a widow from La Porte, Indiana. One of these letters urged Andrew Helgelein to sell his farm in South Dakota and move to La Porte where the two would share the "finest home in northern Indiana."

The fact that Andrew had not mentioned such a venture to his brother was explained by Mrs. Gunness' insistence that their communications be kept a secret. In one letter found in Andrew's effects Belle wrote:

> *But, my dear, please do not say anything about coming here. The surprise will be so much greater when she [Helgelein's sister Anna] finds it out. Now sell all that you can get cash for, and if you have much left you can easily bring it with you whereas we will soon sell it here and get a good price for everything.*

His suspicions now aroused, Asle Helgelein immediately wrote to the La Porte police, who replied that a man fitting his brother's description had indeed been seen in and around town in the company of Mrs. Gunness. A query to Andrew's bank in Aberdeen revealed that money had been sent from his account for collection at the First National Bank of La Porte. A letter from this bank confirmed positively that Andrew, identified by a picture Asle had sent them, had indeed received the money from Aberdeen.

Next, Asle Helgelein had written to Mrs. Gunness herself, who replied in a letter that Andrew had been her guest in January but that he had left her farm to go to Chicago and then perhaps to Norway. In a subsequent reply, Mrs. Gunness reiterated her story, claiming that she was also concerned regarding Andrew's whereabouts and inviting Asle to visit her farm in May. She also reported that a hired hand, "that crazy Lamphere," had been jealous of Andrew and had even stolen some of his letters to her. She confirmed that she had received money from Andrew but claimed that in return she had signed over the deed to her farm to him, a transaction of which no record could later be found.

On May first, Asle received a letter from the First National Bank of La Porte that included a newspaper article concerning the fire and subsequent discovery of four bodies. Alarmed, Helgelein immediately boarded a train that would take him to La Porte.

Now fearing that his brother had been the victim of foul play, the morning after his arrival, Asle met with Sheriff Smutzer, who offered to accompany him to the ruins of the farmhouse. Additionally, the sheriff arranged to have Joseph Maxson, the only survivor of that dreaded night, and another neighbor, Daniel Hutson, meet them at the site. For the bulk of that day, the three searched through the burnt debris for anything that might link Andrew Helgelein to the farm.

On that Monday nothing was found. However, when Asle returned to the farm with Maxson and Hutson the next day, they made a discovery that would change the investigation and La Porte history forever.

As Asle Helgelein later testified, "When I came down onto the road, I was not satisfied, and I went back to the cellar and asked Maxson whether he knew of any hole or dirt having been dug up there about the place early in the spring. He told me he had filled a hole in the garden in March. He did not remember the date. Mrs. Gunness had told him she had the hole dug to put rubbish into it. Mrs. Gunness helped raking, picking up old cans, shoes, and rubbish, and the man, Maxson I think, wheeled it in a wheelbarrow to the hole and dumped it in. I got Maxson to show me the hole, and all three of us started to dig."

The men had dug down only a few feet when all three became conscious of a foul odor emanating from the hole they were excavating. With Maxson speculating that perhaps the odor might be originating from old tomato cans and dead fish dumped into the hole, the men dug further. Within a few feet, however, they made a grisly discovery when a gunnysack was uncovered and removed from the hole. Opening the sack, the three men were shocked and sickened to discover a human neck and arm. Maxson was quickly dispatched to town to summon the sheriff, while the two men remaining covered the hole with a coat and awaited their return. Asle Helgelein had found his brother.

As horrifying as the discovery of the body of Andrew Helgelein was, it would serve as only the beginning of what would soon develop into a crime scene of massive proportions. As the contents of the hole were examined, Maxson noticed another soft spot of earth a few feet away. After examining one of the spots, Sheriff Smutzer ordered the men to dig, and within a few feet, another terrible discovery was made. The men removed the fleshless skeleton of what appeared to be a young girl. Immediately Maxson recalled that Jenny Oleson, Belle Gunness' niece who had lived most of her life with Belle, had disappeared more than a year earlier. Belle had told the household she had "gone away to school" in another state. Peering at the pitiful remains lying on the newly dug earth before them, her story was suddenly cast into deadly doubt.

Nor was this discovery the end. Beneath the spot where the skeleton had lain were the remains of a rotted mattress, and when this was removed, the searchers found what appeared to be human ribs protruding from the earth. Further probing revealed gunnysacks containing the remains of a large man. Digging on, the searchers discovered the skeletons of two small children, each about twelve years old. As darkness fell, the men moved the bodies into an outbuilding where they would stay under guard for the night. Then, Sheriff Smutzer returned to his office to begin calling in more help. What began as an arson inquiry had developed into one of the largest murder investigations in Indiana history.

What occurred over the next several days has become part of the legend of Belle Gunness. As searchers returned to pursue the odious task of examining the farm buildings and grounds for more bodies, word quickly spread throughout the community and state as to what was developing in the sleepy community of La Porte. By May 10, an estimated 15,000 people from across the Midwest flowed into La Porte to view the proceedings. A carnival-like atmosphere pervaded the scene, with at least one vendor selling out his stock of postcards bearing a picture of the gruesome remains of Andrew Helgelein. Other entrepreneurs hawked ice cream and lemonade to the crowd that spread picnic lunches beneath the trees surrounding the farm. The more daring in the throng ventured to the carriage house, which had been appropriated as a temporary morgue, and lifted their children to the windows to peek at the grisly remains laid out there. Several times, the press of the crowd became so unmanageable that the carriage house was finally opened for public viewing of the bodies that had been unearthed from the farm.

Those with the morbid curiosity to walk through the house were rewarded with the sight of a growing number of bodies, most in a state of severe decay. These had been excavated from several holes and soft spots of earth found on the grounds. At least six were removed from one hillside on the farm. Further digging would go on in the hog pens and beneath the foundations of the buildings for several weeks.

Many in the crowd came in hopes of identifying friends or relatives who had disappeared in the area. Matt and Oscar Budsberg arrived from Iola, Wisconsin searching for news of their father, Ole. Like Asle Helgelein, Ole Budsberg had been lured to the Gunness farm through an advertisement in a Norwegian newspaper, appealing for someone to manage a prosperous farm in northwest Indiana. After visiting the farm in March of 1907, he had returned to Wisconsin just long enough to sell his farm and announce to his sons that he was returning to La Porte to stay. It was the last time his sons would see their father until the day they identified his remains in the carriage house of the Gunness farm. During the course of that week, several of the bodies laying in the cloistered darkness of the carriage shed were identified by loved ones.

However, many of the other families who traveled to the Gunness farm did not come away with any more knowledge of their relatives' whereabouts than they had come with. Many of these missing individuals, in all probability, had never been to the Gunness farm to begin with; however, it is possible that many remained at the farm, their remains undiscovered to this day.

In the end, the bodies of twelve men, women, and children were uncovered at the Gunness farm. However, it was popularly conjectured that many more lay beneath the soil around the farm, or perhaps at the bottom of an adjacent pond where Belle had been seen dumping sacks. It was even speculated that Belle had fed the dismembered remains of her victims to the hogs she kept on the grounds. Whatever the case, it can be said that it will never be truly known exactly how many lives had been ended at the hands of Belle Gunness.

When news of the discoveries at the Gunness farm broke into the local and national news, it was immediately understood that the majority of these crimes could not have been the work of Ray Lamphere. At worst, he might have been indicted as an accessory to the murders, a charge that he vehemently denied. Clearly, however, the majority of these crimes had been the work of one woman—Belle Gunness herself.

In the days and weeks after the discovery of the bodies at the Gunness farm, interest began to peak as to just how this seemingly simple widow could have committed such crimes with apparent impunity and exactly how long she had been about her horrific work.

Investigation into the life of Belle Gunness did not answer all these questions, but it did provide some tantalizing details.

The woman who would come to be known as "The Black Widow" was born Brynhild Paulsdeatter Storset on November 11, 1858, in a small town on the west coast of Norway. A simple farm girl, her life seems to have been unremarkable until she set sail for America in September of 1881. Arriving in New York, Brynhild made her way to Chicago, where she moved into a tenement on the 900 block of Francisco Avenue. This was the home of her sister, Mrs. Nellie Larson, who had paid for Brynhild's trip to America.

In Chicago, Brynhild found her time consumed with sewing and laundry work, two of the only economic opportunities available to immigrant women at the time. It can be conjectured that the transition to American life was not as easy for Brynhild as she had hoped, and perhaps in an effort to become more "American," she soon changed her name to "Bella" and became known to friends and neighbors as "Belle."

Her first name was not all that Belle would change. In the late nineteenth century, the Norwegian community in Chicago was a close social group. Somewhere in the mix of new and old immigrants, Belle met Mads Sorrenson, a night watchman and part-time detective. Although official records are difficult to locate, it is known that that the pair married sometime between 1883 and 1889. By 1890 the couple was operating a confectionary store at Grand Avenue and Elizabeth Street. However, apparently this business was not a success, and in 1898, a fire consumed the store. In retrospect, it can be seen that this was the first of a series of mysterious fires that seemed to follow Belle throughout her life.

Insurance money in hand, the Sorrensons moved to Alma Street in the Chicago neighborhood of Auston, where they boarded foster children, as well as possibly having several children of their own. Significantly, at least two of these children seem to have died in mysterious circumstances. Specifically, while the cause of death in each case was listed as "acute colitis," their symptoms were also consistent with poisoning. It should be noted that child mortality in those days was high, and no concrete evidence exists today to indicate that their deaths were murders. However, in light of events that were yet to occur, perhaps these deaths were a precursor of things to come.

In 1900, Mads Sorrenson died suddenly in circumstances that seemed suspicious. While the death certificate issued at the time listed his cause of death as "cerebral hemorrhage," the story was dubious enough to prompt Mads' brother to journey to Chicago from Rhode Island several weeks after the burial and demand that his brother be exhumed and an autopsy performed. His suspicions were based in part on the fact that Mads' symptoms leading to death indicated the possibility of strychnine poisoning. More directly, it was noted that Mads' death occurred on the one day that two of his life insurance policies overlapped. This meant that only in the event of his death on that day would Belle be able to collect from both polices, which she promptly did.

Noting this "coincidental" timing of Mads' death, authorities agreed to exhume and autopsy the body of Sorrenson. While the official results of this autopsy were listed as "inconclusive," it has since been noted that the autopsy did not include the examination of the brain or stomach, which would have been the key for any supposition of poisoning.

However inconclusive the official results might have been, apparently Belle's neighbors and former associates had made their own decision, and Belle found herself suddenly a social outcast in the Norwegian community. Perhaps choosing to escape this stigma, Belle left Chicago to visit a cousin near Fergus Farm, Minnesota. While there, she placed an advertisement in a Chicago newspaper offering to trade her property in Chicago for a farm. Arthur Williams of Chicago responded to this advertisement, and negotiations began on a farm on McClung Road just outside La Porte.

The farm and house had a checkered past. The brick farmhouse that sat on the property at the time had been built in 1877, replacing a cabin that had been built there in 1857. In 1888, the property was purchased by Grosvenor Goss, a local farmer. In the two years he and his family lived on the farm, one family member had committed suicide on the property by hanging. In 1890, Goss sold his farm to C.M. Eddy, a streetcar conductor from Chicago who was searching for the peace and quiet afforded by the rural countryside of Indiana.

However, happiness was not to be his on the property. His wife died within a year of moving to La Porte, and Eddy returned to Chicago where he shortly committed suicide. Upon his death in 1892, the property was sold to Ms. Mattie Altic, who turned the farmhouse into a brothel, catering to travelers through the area.

Even this illicit business did not prosper at the ill-fated property. Altic died suddenly in 1893, and the property was sold several times in the next few years, before Belle Gunness took possession in 1901.

In November of that year, Belle moved onto the farm with three children in her care. The first, a beautiful young girl named Jenny Oleson, had lived with Belle for some years after the death of her mother. Two younger girls, Lucy and Myrtle, shared Belle's last name, and she referred to them as "her own." However, subsequent investigation cast serious doubt on whether or not the two girls were her natural children. Birth certificates listed only a father's name and none for the mother. Moreover, it was widely rumored after her death that over the years Belle had agreed to "adopt" a number of children and, for a fee, raise them to adulthood. Records for such informal agreements do not exist, but if this was the case, then history does not record the whereabouts and fate of these children.

What is known with certainty is that the next spring, another member was added to the family of McClung Road. In April, Belle married Peter Gunness, a widower who had courted her for two months. From outward appearances, the pair seemed happy and well suited to each other. However, like most of the other relationships Belle had developed over the years, this one would come to an abrupt, tragic, and some believe murderous end.

Only eight months after their marriage, Peter Gunness died in a bizarre manner. According to the inquest testimony, Belle claimed that late on Saturday night, after a full day of butchering and making sausage, Gunness had gone to the kitchen to get a pair of shoes that he had left behind the stove to warm. Bending over to pick up the shoes, he had knocked over a pot of hot water on the stove, spilling the scalding water over his head and face. Belle further explained that the pain and shock from his sudden burns cause Gunness to stand up abruptly, knocking a sausage grinder off of a high shelf onto the back of his head, partially crushing his skull.

While an autopsy did show wounds that fit the description given by Belle, her story seemed dubious enough that an inquest was held at the home to seek further details. While many at the time suspected foul play, once again there was a lack of sufficient evidence to bring a charge of murder against Belle, and the inquest ended with an open verdict.

Once again, Belle, her economic welfare bolstered by the life insurance money from Peter Gunness, resumed the life of a widow. Whatever her matrimonial status, however, Belle was far from alone. Within two years of Peter Gunness' death, she placed her first matrimonial ad in a national Norwegian newspaper. This would be the first of many such ads that would be placed in the ensuing years. One such advertisement, a copy of which today resides in the La Porte Historical Museum, reads:

> *Wanted–A woman who owns a beautifully located and valuable farm in first class condition wants a good and reliable man as partner in the same. Some little cash is required for which will be furnished first class security.*

At a time when many Scandinavian men were single or widowed throughout America, such an advertisement must have invited considerable interest. It will never be known how many men wrote to Belle in response. More ominously, perhaps, also unknown is how many made the journey to La Porte, in search of the "first class security" promised. One thing that can be stated categorically is that at least four were murdered, their bodies butchered and then buried on the premises. However, it is popularly conjectured that the actual number of those who perished on the premises is much higher. Speculative counts by historical researchers have ranged from at least fourteen to perhaps as high as forty-eight.

Moreover, it was not simply gentleman suitors who met their end at the Gunness farm. Sadly, as the excavations at the farm continued, the body of the young woman removed from the initial excavation was positively identified as Jenny Oleson. Neighbors recalled that she had disappeared from the farm shortly after she and a local boy seemed to develop a romantic relationship. At the time of her disappearance, Belle had claimed that Jenny had gone east to college. However, a coroner's identification of the remains confirmed that Jenny Oleson had never left her La Porte farm.

Within weeks of the fire at the Gunness home, stories of Belle Gunness and her murderous activity had captured the imagination of the United States and, indeed, the world. Articles concerning her appeared in the newspapers of every city and town in the country, and the international press quickly picked up on the sordid tale of what one English paper referred to as "The American Lady Blue Beard."

Meanwhile, Ray Lamphere still languished in the La Porte county jail for the murder of Belle and her children and the setting of the fire on the farm. Despite his pleas of innocence, it seemed to many that only Ray Lamphere had the motive and opportunity to set the fire that killed the family. It was known that Belle Gunness had publicly accused him of stalking her several times, and only days before the fire Lamphere had reportedly told another local, "I know things about that woman, and she will pay me for it or suffer."

While such evidence might seem to some to provide an open and shut case, in yet another bizarre twist as the investigation continued, a new suspect in the murder of the family and the setting of the fire developed: Belle Gunness herself. Unbelievably, evidence began to come to light that suggested that Belle Gunness had not died in the fire but instead murdered the children as well as another unknown woman to take her place, set the fire, and then made her escape.

Part of the evidence to support such a proposition was the fact that the head of the adult female cadaver was missing when the body was discovered in the basement of the farmhouse after the fire. While some speculated that the skull might have been charred to ashes by the intense heat, others noted that the other bodies in the basement, though badly burned, had remained intact.

Another fact that fueled this speculation was the fact that the body of the woman found in the basement was considerably smaller than Belle had been in life. This led to a contentious and inconclusive debate among officials as to whether this "shrinkage" could be accounted for by the heat itself.

Those who supposed Belle to be alive also pointed to her actions in the days before the fire. One neighbor reported seeing Belle drive past her farm several days earlier with an unknown woman in her carriage. It was noted that the woman, who was dressed in traveling attire, was considerably smaller in stature than Belle. She was never seen again.

The day before the fire, Belle Gunness had gone into town, withdrawn part of her savings from a local bank, and purchased five gallons of kerosene oil. Such actions, which seemed innocent at the time, took on more ominous and sinister implications in light of subsequent events.

As news of the possibility that Belle Gunness might still be alive leaked into the press, suddenly a glut of Belle Gunness sightings erupted across the nation. One matronly lady, bound for New York to visit family, told of being removed from her train and questioned by local authorities for several hours because a fellow passenger had reported her the railroad officials for her resemblance to Belle Gunness. Other reports came from California, Florida, and from as far away as Norway and Paris. None, however, ever proved to be the elusive Black Widow.

Meanwhile, the one person who perhaps could have cleared up this mystery seemed to be giving contradictory stories regarding the fate of Belle Gunness. From his cell in the La Porte County Jail, Ray Lamphere refused to officially reveal anything he knew regarding her whereabouts. However, several people were to later claim that Lamphere did confide what he knew to them. A cellmate alleged that he had talked of picking up Gunness in a carriage at her home in the early morning hours of that fated day and taking her to a train station in the next town.

Another man claimed that Lamphere had told him in a jailhouse interview that he had indeed killed Belle, but accidentally. According to this story, Lamphere and a compatriot had gone to the Gunness house that night to rob Belle of money he felt she owed him. Using chloroform to drug her during the robbery, he had accidentally overdosed her and caused her death. Thus, he had no choice but to kill the children and start the fire to cover up his crimes.

Many other stories were told in the local and national press, all attributed to Ray Lamphere and often written by authors with little or no real connection to the case. Before and during his trial, Lamphere officially maintained his innocence and claimed to have no knowledge of the fate of Belle Gunness.

The trial itself lived up to the hype that surrounded it. On November 9, 1908, the trial of Ray Lamphere began in the La Porte courtroom of Judge J.C. Richter. On November 13, with the jury picked and seated, prosecutor Ralph Smith made his opening statement before the jurors, judge, and a packed courtroom of almost 500 people. It was his promise, he said, to prove beyond any doubt that Belle Gunness had died by fire and that it was Ray Lamphere who, out of revenge, had set the fire.

For the next week, a parade of prosecution witnesses testified, trying to tie Lamphere inexorably to the apparent death of Belle Gunness. However, Lamphere's defense attorney, Wirt Worden, managed to cast the shadow of doubt on most of their testimonies. By the time the prosecution rested its case, most spectators and reporters present called the trial a dead heat.

On Friday, November 20, the defense opened its argument, promising to remove all doubt that Belle Gunness was not dead. To back this promise, Worden then produced a number of witnesses, mostly neighbors, who claimed specifically to having seen Belle Gunness alive after the fire. One Daniel Hutson, claimed that on July 9 he had seen Belle Gunness walking in her orchard with an unknown man. When he approached the pair, intending to apprehend Gunness, the two had run to their buggy, parked nearby, and raced away. Hutson's two daughters then took the stand to testify that they, too, had seen Gunness in the vicinity of her property on two separate occasions in early July.

While the prosecutor, Smith, did his best to shake the stories of these witnesses, it seemed as though the damage was done. On November 25, the jury began their deliberation. Two days later, word was sent to Judge Richter that they had arrived at a verdict. As word quickly spread, the courtroom became crowded with reporters and spectators. Clearly, some were there expecting to hear Ray Lamphere convicted of all charges and sentenced to death. Perhaps an equal number expected him to be exonerated of all charges. Both camps were to be disappointed.

When the jury foreman read the verdict, Lamphere was convicted simply of arson and acquitted of murder. However, in a strange footnote to the proceedings, the jury foreman then read a statement from the jury stating that it was their belief that the woman found dead in the basement was indeed Belle Gunness and that the case had been decided on "an entirely different proposition."

Whatever their motivation, the jury had spared the life of Ray Lamphere. He was sentenced to "between two and twenty years" in the state penitentiary and was led from the courtroom. However, this was to be far from the end of the mystery of Belle Gunness.

Lamphere was taken to the state prison in Michigan City the next day. It is said that as he first viewed the imposing walls of the penitentiary, he quipped to a guard, "I am better off here than I would be if I were with her." As significant and enigmatic as such a statement might be, it would not be his last with regard to Gunness. During his stay at the prison, Lamphere is said to have often spoken about the woman who had caused his downfall.

His cellmate, Harry Myers, reported that often Lamphere would stare idly out their window at the free world outside and then mutter, "She's out there, Harry." Myers also reported that one day, observing a woman passing through the courtyard below their window, Lamphere remarked to him, "She's about the size of my old gal. People think that she's dead. She's not dead..." According to Myers, Lamphere then paused for a moment while still gazing out the window and then continued, "I know where Belle is, and she's not far from here, believe me."

The truth of Lamphere's statement will never be known. His stay at the Michigan City State Prison was brief; a little over a year after entering the facility he died of liver failure. With him died the last hope the world had of definitely discovering the fate of Belle Gunness.

For many years afterward, Belle Gunness sightings were reported in the popular press from all across the nation. None, however, could be proven to be the infamous "Black Widow." One particularly intriguing possibility came in 1931, when a seventy-one year-old woman going by the name of Esther Carlson was arrested in Los Angeles for the poisoning murder of a man for whom she was caring. It is also known that Ms. Carlson was under investigation in that city for the deaths of several other men by similar means. According to one press report, when investigators examined a trunk found in her room, they found, lying at the bottom, a picture of Belle Gunness with three of her children.

As fate would have it, Ms. Carlson died in jail before she could stand trial and before any connection between her and Belle Gunness could be ascertained. However, two former residents of La Porte, then living in Los Angeles, were allowed to view her body at the morgue and are said to have come away convinced that the body they saw there was that of the woman they had known as Belle Gunness.

While the death of Esther Carlson does not represent the final chapter in the story of Belle Gunness, it is one of a seemingly endless sea of intriguing possibilities. Indeed, the life, crimes, and eventual fate of Belle Gunness are as much open to speculation as they were that dark morning when flames engulfed the farmhouse on the outskirts of La Porte. The legend of Belle Gunness truly lives on.

However, for those in the vicinity of McClung Road, it is whispered that perhaps the legend of Belle Gunness is not the only thing she has left behind. As one researcher has noted, "Residents say that old McClung Road reeks with her aura; one expects her to materialize from behind the old house that still faces the same cornfields just outside of town." Perhaps it is this very aura of murder, horror, and mystery that explains some of the odd tales told in the area and some of the enigmatic experiences that have been encountered by the young family that today lives in the dwelling built on the foundation of the Gunness farmhouse.

After fire engulfed the home on that fated morning, the property on which it stood changed hands several times over the ensuing decades. Owners seemed reluctant to build a home on land with such a horrifying past, but by the mid-1930s, perhaps the memories had faded enough that a brick home was built over the foundation and basement left of the Gunness home. In the late 1980s, a second story was added to expand the living area. Today, the house that sits quietly on the spot of so much horror and death seems quiet and sedate, with no hint of its history. However, if the stories told are to be believed, then perhaps the spirits of this home, like the story of Belle itself, are not quite gone.

In 2000, John and Betty Matula* moved into the quaint home on McClung Road. For some time they had been searching for a larger home to accommodate their growing family, and Betty says that when she first saw the house she immediately fell in love with it. Even the discovery of the sordid history of the house was not enough to dissuade them from their decision to purchase it.

As Betty recalls, the day they came to make an offer on the house, their real estate agent took John aside to reveal the history of the home. "When we left the house, she was by her vehicle, and she asked John to come over and she was whispering something to him. I walked up and she was telling him that there was history to the house and what that history was, and so I asked her to tell me the whole story. I think she was afraid that we were going to back out on our offer, but when she was done telling the story, I just said 'Let's go—I don't care who died here, I still want that house!'"

A month later, John and Betty moved into their new home with their three children, aged eight, five, and three. While they admit to hearing the odd creaking of the stair at night or being slightly "spooked" by the trees brushing against the house on a windy evening, basically, John and Betty, along with their children, seem to be very happy in their new home. However, there have been several incidents that have made them question if they are alone in the house.

Their first hint of something odd came shortly after they moved to the property when their youngest son began talking to "imaginary friends." While many youngsters have imaginary friends, there was something about his reactions to these friends that gave Betty Matula pause.

"A month or two after we moved in, he started establishing these imaginary friends," she now recalls. "At first I thought nothing of it. He would be in his bedroom playing, and would start having this conversation with himself. Watching him, I would say, 'Who are you talking to?' and he would reply, 'I am talking to the monster.' I thought, well, OK. Then, the next time he would be talking to 'the ghost,' and then 'the boy,' or 'the man.' There were five or six of them," she continues.

"He would just walk through the house, and talk to them and laugh at whatever they were doing. It got to be a little strange. It really started bothering me when he wanted to involve me in the conversations he was having with these imaginary friends. The first time I was picking up toys in his room, and he was standing just outside the door in the living room, and he said, 'Mom, the ghost wants to say something to you.' I said, 'OK, I but can't hear the ghost, so what does the ghost want to say?' My son looked at me and said, 'He just wants to say that he likes you.' I said, 'OK, you tell him I like him, too,' but then he added, 'But, Mom, don't ever, ever try to hurt him because he'll get mad. Someone hurt him before, and if you try to hurt him he'll be mad.' Something about that last part bothered me. I said, 'OK!' but I was thinking, 'I don't like that.'"

Betty also recalls other details concerning her son's imaginary friends that she found disconcerting. One was his description of one whom he named 'the man.' "One day he was talking to The Man, and I asked him what he looked like," Betty recalls. "He smiled and said that he looked funny—that he was brown all over. All I could think of was someone who had died in a fire, or whose body had been burned in a fire like the people in the basement."

Another seemingly insignificant aspect of these imaginary friends was related to the friend he called 'the boy.' Betty explains that when she asked her son how he came to meet this friend, he told her that he met him one day by the fence toward the back of the property. "He was crying," the boy told his mother, "because someone had tried to hurt him." Betty goes on to point out that the fence in question is directly in front of the area where searchers had unearthed human remains of both adults and children.

Other strange things have happened in the house that have given the Matulas pause. One is the odd behavior of several electronic devices. "We have a couple of computers in the house, and both of them have been known to turn themselves on," John relates. "I always turn the computer off in our room before we go to bed at night," he continues. "Then, in the middle of the night, it will turn itself back on. It will come back on and start playing music in the middle of the night. This has probably happened half a dozen times since we have lived in the house. Then, when we had painters working in the living room, they said that they saw the computer there do it, too."

The painters in question seemed to have witnessed a number of strange events. Their presence in the home was due to a fire that occurred in February 2002. At the time, the Matulas were doing refinishing work in the house and sanding wood in the basement.

"At the time, knowing that Belle Gunness had apparently set a couple of fires in the places she lived and that our basement was the only part of the original house," John recalls with a chuckle, "my wife kidded me by saying 'Oh, she's out to get you!' But there was a logical explanation. There was sawdust all over the place in the basement, and we were storing some rags and refinishing solution, and after a couple of days, we just had spontaneous combustion. It really did not burn up much but there was smoke damage throughout the house. We had to move out for several weeks while the workmen repainted and cleaned the place up."

According to Betty, while working in the home, the painters reported several incidents that were odd to say the least. One of these concerned a large screen television in an upstairs family room that turned itself on several times during their time there.

"Apparently, they would walk into the room and the TV would be on," John says with a smile. "They would turn it off, but a few minutes later it would turn itself on again. The funny thing is that it has never done that for us."

The painters also described to the Matulas hearing a radio turn itself off and on as well as having some of their tools mysteriously misplaced while working in the home, only to have them later reappear in a spot they had previously searched. None of these incidents, however, could compare to one episode the shaken workmen reported to Betty Matula. "I came into the house every morning to chat with the workmen," Betty relates, "and to see how things were going. They were really into the whole 'Belle Gunness thing,' and they were constantly telling me about things they said had gone on there."

"One morning," she continues, "they told me that the day before, one of the workmen had been on a ladder leaning up against the wall in the family room. He had been in there for a while looking up at what he was doing, and at one point another workman came in and looked up to see how he was doing. He swore that when he looked up at him, the ladder was no longer leaning against the wall—he said it was kind of floating out from the wall several inches, while the man on the ladder had no idea that it was happening. Then it just sort of gently floated back down."

Perhaps the Matulas are not the only ones who sense an odd aura to the home on McClung Road. John and Betty report that their small dog steadfastly refuses to climb down the steps to the basement of the home, even if his owners call to him. At other times the friendly pet has been known to sit at the top of the stairs and peer downward, barking furiously toward a seemingly empty basement. It should be noted that this basement is the only area of the home still left from the farmhouse owned by Belle Gunness as well as being the site where the first bodies were recovered after the fire there.

Despite the odd occurrences that periodically transpire at the home, neither John or Betty, nor their young children, seem to feel the least bit uncomfortable there. "Do I believe this house is haunted?" Betty muses, "I really don't know. I believe it is possible, but if it is, there is nothing here that wants us out or wants to hurt us in any way. I have never felt threatened at all."

As strange as the Matulas' incidents may seem, they are not the only ones who have encountered odd happenings on and near the property. According to one report, a neighbor has claimed that passing by the property one evening some time ago, she glimpsed the figure of a woman walking behind the home where Belle Gunness once dug holes to bury her "rubbish." According to the story, the figure was that of a heavy-set woman in a long, old-fashioned dress. When approached, the figure seemed to evaporate into the gathering dusk.

Another strange tale is told by Ronald Bemmer,* a retired La Porte police officer. As he reports, he was patrolling the outskirts of the town late one night in the mid-1970s when he spotted a car passing him going the opposite direction at a high rate of speed. "They passed me doing at least 60," Bemmer now recalls, "and I turned around quickly and put on my lights. As they pulled over, I could see they were a car load of teenagers, and I assumed they were just a bunch of kids on a joy ride."

As he pulled over and approached the car, however, he quickly realized that this was not a standard traffic stop. "I got up to the car, ready to write a ticket," he now recalls, "but when I shone my light in the car, I could see that the kids were in a panic. This was not the usual kind of intimidation that kids had in those days when pulled over by a cop. I mean these kids were literally shaking."

Both concerned and suspicious, the officer asked the young people to come to his car, and when there, he asked them where they were going and what explanation they could offer for their high rate of speed. By now, somewhat calmer but still clearly rattled, one of the boys blurted, "We were just going anywhere we could to get away from her."

Haltingly, and after much questioning, the teenagers revealed their story. As Officer Bemmer now remembers it, they told him that they had gone out for the evening with nothing particular to do. Somewhat bored, one of them suggested that they drive out to McClung Road and find the Belle Gunness property to 'see if they could scare up a few spooks.' "I think one of them said they had done a report for school on Belle Gunness," Bemmer says, "and her mother had taken her past the property, so she had a pretty good idea of where to go." After a bit of driving and a few wrong turns, the teens found the home and pulled into the drive, noting that the house was dark and apparently devoid of human habitation.

Bemmer continues that after a some good natured laughter and a bit of daring one another, three of the four left their car and walked toward the back of the property, climbing over the short fence at the end of the driveway. Though dark, Bemmer remembers that there was a full moon hanging in the sky, and by its illumination, the intrepid teenagers made their way toward the back of the property.

As they later related the story to Officer Bemmer, their explorations were suddenly cut short by a sound that seemed to tear through the very air around them. "They told me that suddenly they heard a scream—a man's scream. They said it sounded like someone was in agony. Then they said they heard a thud, like the sound of a body hitting the ground." Startled, one of the young people let out a scream of her own, and all three turned to make a hasty escape back to the safety of their car.

However, according their tale, as they turned and began to make their retreat, they were confronted with a more unsettling sight. "These kids said that as they turned to run, they all saw, standing about ten feet away, the figure of a tall woman. They said they could not make out her features in the moonlight, but they all swore that she was heavy set and wore an old-fashioned dress. They told me that she just stood there motionless for a minute, and then they heard her laugh. They said it was a sadistic, almost maniacal laugh."

With fear now turning to panic, all three ran toward their car, two simply vaulting the fence they had climbed moments before. The third, however, was not as lucky and fell climbing over, sustaining a scrape to the knee later shown to Officer Bemmer as evidence of the truth of their tale. Undeterred by the minor injury, the young man in question quickly regained his footing and joined his friends at the car. Throwing himself into the back seat as the driver put the car in gear, the four headed back to town at a speed that had caught the attention of the patrolling officer.

On the face of it, the tale told to Officer Bemmer sounded very much like a classic teenage adventure story, the sort of which is told and embellished in every school in America. However, according to Officer Bemmer, an experienced law enforcement professional, there was something about this story that gave him pause.

"I was a police officer for thirty-three years," Officer Bemmer now says with the hint of a smile. "Most of that time I was on the road; I have pulled over a great many drivers, including a lot of teenagers. I have heard every conceivable crazy story that you can imagine to try and get out of a ticket. However, the thing I remember most about what these kids said was the fear on their faces. That, you can't fake. They were literally shaking, and they seemed almost glad I pulled them over. I think it made them feel safer to be talking to a policeman. I also took the time that night to question them each individually about what they had seen and heard, and they all told the exact same story."

In the end, Officer Bemmer chose to let the young people go simply with an admonition to slow down and stay away from private property, especially at night. "I did not have the heart to give them a ticket," the retired policeman now recalls. "They were just too shook up. To tell you the truth, I have no idea what happened to those kids that night. You can write the whole thing off to adolescent imagination, I guess, but this much I do believe, whatever they saw or heard, it scared them plenty. That I can promise you."

If one listens to the tales that are told in La Porte and its surrounding community, one knows that such tales are not uncommon. While few can be confirmed and authenticated, they are nevertheless an indelible piece of local folklore and a part of the historical fabric of the region.

In the town of La Porte, the legend of Belle Gunness lives on. A tale that began with a spark of flame early in the last century in an anonymous Indiana farmhouse has grown and blossomed into one of the darkest and most horrific chapters in the annals of American crime. Belle Gunness has gone from being a simple Hoosier widow to the most prolific female serial killer in American history. Her life, crimes, and the questions about her eventual fate have all become part of her legend.

With the passing of time, the town of La Porte has moved on and become a thoroughly modern Indiana city. However, even today, the name of Belle Gunness is whispered in hushed and almost reverential tones in the area. It is almost as though this Black Widow, whose day has long since passed, still casts her dark shadow across the Indiana countryside where she once perpetuated her murderous pursuits. And nowhere can this shadow be more keenly felt than in the rustic environs of McClung Road.

It should be noted that, despite the sordid history of the homestead, the dwelling sitting quietly amid the tall trees seems very much like a pleasant, normal suburban home. Those who reside there are a healthy, happy family, content and comfortable with their home. Perhaps peace has finally come to the homestead on McClung Road.

However, on dark nights when the wind whispers among the overhanging trees and the leaves rustle where once a sinister woman buried mysterious bundles, the questions remain. For, in some way, perhaps it is possible that a part of Belle Gunness has remained here—as a dark chapter of Hoosier legend and a mysterious part of Indiana ghostlore.

5
THE SPIRITS OF THE OLD COUNTY JAIL
VALPARAISO

In jail a man has no personality. He is a minor disposal problem and a few entries on reports. Nobody cares who loves or hates him, what he looks like, what he did with his life. Nobody reacts to him unless he gives trouble. Nobody abuses him. All that is asked of him is that he goes quietly to the right cell and remains quiet when he gets there. There is nothing to fight against, nothing to be mad at. The jailers are quiet men without animosity or sadism. All this stuff you read about men yelling and screaming, beating against the bars, running spoons along them, guards rushing in with clubs—all that is for the big house. A good jail is one of the quietest places in the world....Life in jail is in suspension.

—Raymond Chandler

When thinking of the word "jail," many images come to mind. Perhaps it is the picture of solemn, disheveled prisoners languishing endless hours behind grim iron bars or the cold, sterile environment of a modern day "lockup," yet it is undeniable that our local jails evoke strong emotions and perhaps even horror in most law-abiding citizens.

From time immemorial, society has had the need for a place to separate those who have violated the laws of that community from the general populace. Whether for simple punishment, or hopefully for rehabilitation, we have always had need for places of incarceration. While many of us may intentionally give little thought to such places, they serve an important, albeit regrettable, place in the civilized world.

While we may not consider it, there is much of the drama of life within the confines of our local jails. Tragedy, desperation, and even redemption are all a part of the day-to-day existence in our jail systems. While many may view life behind bars as being the darkest kind of human experience, it is, nonetheless, a part of the drama of that lies just beneath the seeming civility of our society.

Perhaps this explains why, as some believe, a residue of that substance remains in many jails long after the prisoners have departed this mortal existence. Indeed, a review of ghostly tales from across the United States reveals numerous stories of historic haunted jails and prisons. Some are eerie tales of justice denied and retribution exacted from beyond the grave. Others are of a more benign nature.

Indiana can count at least three ghostly accounts related to former jails. Perhaps one of the best documented is the historic Old County Jail in Valparaiso, now home to the Jail Museum and Historical Society of Porter County.

Sitting serenely to one side of the beautiful town square, the sturdy old building has seen much of the history of Valparaiso and all of Porter County. The oldest section of what is now the Old County Jail Museum was built in the 1860s as a private residence. In the early 1870s, the home was purchased by Porter County as a home for the county sheriff, and an addition was added to house a small jail. For the next 103 years, the site served as the Porter County Jail.

During that time, renovations and additions were made to the facility. In 1947, a second story was added to the jail section including a dorm-style lockup for women and juveniles. At the same time, a cell was added in the basement area that served as a "drunk tank." Reputedly, before this time, the area was used for holding the mentally handicapped or unstable who were judged unable to be housed with other prisoners.

While these additions were undertaken to accommodate a rising flow of prisoners, reflective of the increasing population of the county, it can be seen that even these additions were insufficient. The official number of prisoners that could be accommodated in the jail was raised to thirty-two, but by the time of its closure some twenty-seven years later, over 100 prisoners were crammed into the inadequate space.

In 1974, a new jail, more spacious and modern, was completed, and the venerable old jail was apparently vacated of its prisoners. At that time, the building was offered to the Porter County Historical Society who refurbished the jail as a museum. While today the jail houses a variety of historical memorabilia spanning the history of Porter County, it still maintains its original character. The residential area where the sheriffs and their families lived during their time in office still contains vintage antiques and other artifacts. It seems ironic that, just a few feet away from this gracious section, visitors are confronted with the spartan living conditions that were experienced by those incarcerated there.

The upper floor of the jail now houses historical collections that have been donated chiefly from local residents. It also contains meeting space and storage for the museum and jail cells that have been kept in their original condition. Overall, to step into the Old County Jail Museum is to step back into a fascinating piece of Porter County history. The very ambiance of the place speaks of the drama that has been played out within its walls for over 130 years.

Perhaps this explains the tales that have been whispered for many years—stories that suggest that the sagas of some of those who inhabited the jail may not have ended when the curtain fell on their earthly lives. These are macabre accounts told by those who believe that not all the inmates of the old jail obtained their eternal parole.

One who tells such stories is Teresa Schmidt, the current manager of the Old County Jail Museum. Displaying an energetic, no-nonsense character, Ms. Schmidt does not seem a person one would pick to be the bearer of ghostly tales, yet in speaking with her of her experiences, one is quickly impressed with her earnestness.

Ms. Schmidt began her association with the museum in 2001 and quickly immersed herself in the history of the building and the artifacts it now houses. At the time of her arrival at the jail, she had no knowledge of the spectral inhabitants said to lurk there. However, all this began to change with the passage of time.

"About two weeks after I started working here," she now relates, "a coworker, Shirron, and I were on the first floor early one Wednesday morning. It was before we opened, and no one was there but the two of us. As we sat and talked, we heard a sound from the second floor. It sounded like someone had taken a button and just skipped it across the hall of the jail overhead. We heard it clearly—not just once but several times. Finally, we went upstairs, but no one was there, and there was nothing on the floor."

As trivial as this incident might seem, it would not be the last time Teresa would hear the sound. In the coming months, she and her co-workers would witness the enigmatic noises on several occasions.

A partial explanation to the mystery occurred several months later when Ms. Schmidt happened to meet an elderly gentleman who told her that he had worked at the jail for many years as a guard. Sensing a possible source of information, Teresa questioned the man at some length for stories of what life had been like at the jail during his tenure there.

"In the course of our conversation," Teresa remembers, "he told me that it was common for prisoners, if they wanted to pass information from one cell to another but did not want to be overheard, to tie notes to small stone marbles and skip them down the hallway from cell to cell. As soon as I heard that, I realized that this was the sound I had been hearing. I also realized that a few weeks before I had been unpacking some boxes of jail artifacts and had found a couple of stones that fit that description exactly.

"I was kind of excited to share this story after talking with the man, so as soon as I got back to the museum, I told Shirron what I had heard. Then I told her about finding the stones in the boxes and took her upstairs to show them to her. I specifically remember that when I had originally found them, I had put them in a bookcase upstairs so that I would know

photo courtesy of Chris Shultz

Exterior of Old County Jail Museum, Valparaiso

where they were, but when I took Shirron up there, they were gone. I asked around, and no one knew anything about the stones and no one had moved them. They had just vanished."

Interestingly, many months later the stones were found again in a separate part of the museum by another staff member, and today the stones are on exhibit in the second floor museum section of the jail. However, the unexplained reappearance of these objects has not lessened the mystery of the skipping sounds that are still frequently heard today by staff members of the museum.

As strange as these sounds might be, they are by no means the only spectral noises that are said to echo through the halls of the jail at odd moments. Ms. Schmidt has heard other, more disturbing sounds.

"It seems to happen most often when we are alone or when things are being moved around in the museum," Ms. Schmidt reflects. "Once last year, a coworker and I were moving exhibits from one room to another upstairs when we heard this clanging sound—like someone beating on a pipe or metal bar. It sounded like it was coming from directly below us. It would go and then stop and then start up again. I had been here long enough to know about every sound this place can make, and I had never heard anything like this before.

"We checked and could not find anything that would cause the banging so we went back to work. What was interesting, though, was that as we moved from room to room, the sound would follow us. It would be in whatever room we were in at that moment. It was like someone was trying to get our attention."

On another occasion, Ms. Schmidt was to witness an even more eerie and chilling auditory phenomena that has left a lasting impression on her. "It was just before Christmas of 2001, and it was the end of the day," she remembers. "I was the last one here, and I was at the back of the first floor by the circuit breaker turning off the lights in the jail."

As Teresa prepared to leave the building, she was stopped short by a sound that seemed to emanate through the floorboard below and filled the air around her. "It was a groan—a human groan, like someone in intense pain or anguish. It was horrible. I literally thought, 'That's it—I'm out of here.' I shut off the lights and left quickly."

As Ms. Schmidt reflects on the origin of this sound, she draws an even more eerie conjecture. "The sound seemed to come from directly below me, which is the area where they had the drunk tank. This is just a hunch, but maybe they used to put people who were mentally incapacitated or unbalanced down there in shackles. It was a typical thing to do back then. When I think about it, it still gets to me."

Another seemingly common auditory experience that Theresa and many who have worked at the museum have shared is hearing muffled voices speaking in the house when no one was present. "I have often heard people whispering—we all have," she reflects. "It is ongoing, especially at the end of the day when everyone has cleared out and you are shutting things down."

Teresa describes the phenomena as more than one voice in a muffled conversation. The sounds have been heard throughout the museum, particularly, she notes, when visitors are not in the building. "They sound like they are in another part of the house or maybe even just outside the room you are in at that moment," she explains. "It is kind of like they are whispering or talking in very low tones so you can't understand what they're saying. Recently, a group of us were on the main floor when we heard voices coming from the hallway. Someone looked at me and said, 'Is there anyone else here?' and I had to tell him we were alone. After a few minutes we went into the hall, but there was no one there."

Ms. Schmidt's experience at the old jail has not been limited to simply auditory phenomena. On several occasions she has seen things that seem to defy explanation. She describes an episode that occurred in October of 2002 when the jail museum was opened as a commercial "Haunted House" for Halloween. "As we were setting up for the haunted house," she says, "we covered a doorway with black felt so that it was darkened. I was upstairs in the stairway looking down at Shirron who was down at the bottom of the stairs, and the drape behind her started moving back and forth. I said, 'Shirron, they're aware of what we are doing—I don't know if they like it or not, but they are aware of it.' As soon as I said it, the curtain just went to a dead stop."

Perhaps the most dramatic sighting reported by Teresa Schmidt was of the shadowy figure of a man that she has seen on several occasions in the upstairs meeting room. "We were going to have a meeting late one afternoon," she now recalls. "We were cleaning the committee room and getting it ready when I happened to glance at one old chair that sits at the end of the table. It is a large chair with arms; it almost looks like a throne." While Ms. Schmidt had seen the chair many times during the course of her duties at the museum, what attracted her attention on this occasion was the fact that this time it seemed to be occupied. Teresa says that she could see a misty figure now seated in the space that had been vacant a moment before. "It was hazy—you couldn't make out any facial features;" she recalls, "you could just tell he had broad shoulders and was probably tall. He was sitting in this chair, not moving, while I looked on from the other end of the table. I looked again to make sure that I was not imagining things, and then I turned to my coworker, Shirron, and said, 'Let's go downstairs for a while,' and that is what we did." Since that time, she reports having seen the same figure in that room on at least two other occasions.

Interestingly, Ms Schmidt believes that there is not one but several ghostly presences in the old jail. "There is a lady in the downstairs section of the house. I haven't seen her, but several other people have. We constantly have school groups coming through here, and several times we have had children, who have no idea of the stories, talk about the lady they saw downstairs in an old-fashioned long dress." Needless to note, staff at the museum do not normally wear period clothing, and no logical explanation could be made for the reported sightings. Nor is the phantom woman in the downstairs section the final note on ghostly happenings at the museum.

"There is also at least one person in one of the upstairs bedrooms, in what we call the rope bedroom," Ms. Schmidt continues. "That is one room that I did not feel comfortable in from the day I got here. We also believe that there is a child in the children's bedroom upstairs. No one has ever seen her, but things have been moved around in that room when no one was there. Every year we decorate that room for Christmas. We put up stockings on the mantle in that room, and every single day, we come in to find all but one of the stockings down on the floor. There is just one left up. It happens every year."

Perhaps one of the most bizarre phantoms reported is that of a dog who is said to be present in the museum both spiritually and physically. "We have a stuffed dog in the downstairs section of the museum," Teresa notes. "It is a strange artifact, I'll grant you. It came to us from the estate of a family in the area who had this dog that they loved very much. When the dog died in 1916, they took its body to the Field Museum and had the taxidermist stuff it so they could still have the dog in the house."

As unusual and even macabre as the idea may sound today, such a practice was not unusual in the early days of the twentieth century. However strange the practice may be, more unusual still are the events reported by staff members after the stuffed artifact was donated to the museum several years ago. "I have caught glimpses of a dog that looks just like that dog wandering through the museum," Teresa reports. "I have also frequently heard barking when no one is around. Once I was vacuuming the main floor when I was alone, and the barking was so loud that I turned off the vacuum cleaner and searched the house. Also, and this happens fairly frequently, I will be walking through the house and feel something that feels just like a dog brush by my leg. It is like he is just letting me know he is there, that's all."

This is not the only ghostly tale attributed to the museum that centers not around the building itself but instead seems attached to a donated artifact housed there. Another fascinating tale related to a museum exhibit is told by Kevin Pazour, a young man who recently completed a student internship at the museum in preparation for his college studies. As part of the duties of his internship, Kevin was frequently called upon to take artifacts from the museum to local schools to give presentations to students on Porter County history.

As Pazour tells the story, "One time I went to a local school on a Friday and I took along several of the artifacts that had been donated to the jail. One of them was a World War I soldier's helmet. It is a unique piece because you can see entrance and exit holes in the helmet where a bullet had apparently gone through it. Also, the helmet lining is not with the piece, which is, historically, a telltale sign that the person wearing the helmet had been killed."

The parlor of the Old County Jail Museum

photo courtesy of Chris Shultz

"Since my talk was on a Friday and the museum did not open again till Wednesday," Mr. Pazour continues, "I had to bring the artifacts back to my parents' house for the weekend. I put the artifacts, including the helmet, in my room, and as I turned to go I saw this bright light out of the corner of my eye. It was there and then gone. I thought it was odd but then forgot about it."

However, as the weekend wore on his attention was repeatedly drawn to brief flashes of light that seemed to follow him from room to room. "At one point, I was alone in the house when I came out of the bathroom and saw a light coming from underneath my bedroom door. I thought maybe I had forgotten to turn off the light, but when I opened the door, I discovered that there was no light on. At that point, I decided to take the helmet back to the museum and never take it out again."

True to his decision, Kevin returned the helmet to the museum early Monday morning and began to regale a staff member with his account of the odd events at his home the previous weekend. "As we sat at the table, I was talking about what had happened," he remembers. "As I was telling the story, I picked up the helmet and was kind of absent-mindedly running my thumb lightly over the bullet entry hole, and I noticed it was suddenly hot. I thought, 'That's weird!' and put my thumb over the hole, and it was suddenly so hot that when I jerked my hand away it was blistered. It was strange, to say the least."

This strange account was not the first of Mr. Pazour's mysterious encounters at the jail. As he recalls, his first brush with the uncanny occurred shortly after beginning his internship there.

"I started working at the museum in February of 2001. The first time I came here I thought the old place looked a little spooky, so I asked someone, 'Is this place haunted?' and they kind of passed off my question with a quick 'No,' so I didn't think any further of it," he now remembers. However, this seemingly innocent question would soon come back to haunt him.

"Within the first few days of working here, one of the staff gave me a thorough tour of the place. Toward the end of the tour we were in the basement—the old drunk tank. They were showing me the old window and how the brick was laid around it, when out of the corner of my eye I caught sight of a figure standing a few feet from us."

Kevin recalls that he could not see the face of the murky figure nor could he see the lower body. "It was like the head and shoulders and the upper portion of the torso, but then it kind of faded out below that. I quickly turned toward the figure; it seemed to turn away, and then suddenly it was just gone."

From that time until the end of his internship in August 2003, Kevin Pazour reports experiencing a number of strange phenomena within the walls of the Old County Jail. "Mostly it was a lot of little things," he now recalls. "You would put something on a table or counter and come back a moment later to find it gone. Later it would turn up somewhere else, where you knew you did not leave it. Several times I have seen the keys hanging on the key rack start to swing back and forth of their own volition and then suddenly stop, only to begin their mysterious movements again a moment later. And then there are the voices…"

Like Teresa Schmidt, Kevin reports frequently hearing voices in the empty rooms of the museum at odd times of the day when no other human occupants were in the building. "I have heard whole conversations—both men's and women's voices. Upstairs in the jail section, it is always men's voices, but in the house section I have heard women, too." Interestingly, also like Ms. Schmidt, Kevin reports that while he definitely could hear the voices, they seemed strangely hushed and no particular words could be picked out. Perhaps sounds, muted by the passage of time, are still intruding into the present day.

Kevin also notes that his inexplicable experience with the World War I helmet was not his only encounter with a museum artifact that seems to possess a life of its own. At one point, a few months after coming to the Old County Jail, he was asked to look at an antique typewriter that was to be used in a special exhibit.

"We were working on an exhibit of local newspaper history, and there was one that seemed to be in perfect condition except for the fact that the keys were not working. It was like something was stopping them from being pressed," he now recalls. "They asked me to take a look at it, so I went upstairs and tried everything I knew to get the thing working. I pounded on the keys to see if I could get them unstuck and even flipped the typewriter over to see if there was some sort of a lock on it, but I couldn't get the keys to move.

"After a little bit I turned away from the typewriter to look at the book that came with it," Kevin continues. "We were lucky enough to not only have this vintage typewriter but also the cover and original manual, and I decided to see if there was anything in the manual that could help me. Anyway, as I turned away from the typewriter, which was sitting on a file cabinet, suddenly, the typewriter started typing all by itself. I spun around to look at the typewriter, and the keys were moving all by themselves. It probably typed six or eight letters and then stopped. I just shook my head, took the typewriter downstairs and from then on the keys did not stick anymore," he concludes.

One of Mr. Pazour's most unnerving experiences, however, came in August of 2003, when he came to open the museum in preparation for a visit by the Indiana Ghost Trackers, a local ghost research group. As he relates the story, he was alone in the building and was walking through the parlor area when he was stopped short by the sight of a woman standing in the room. "I couldn't see her face," he says, "but it was the figure of a woman in an old-fashioned dress standing next to the old Victrola by the window. I clearly saw her, but I looked away quickly in shock, and when I looked back, she was gone."

Not believing his senses, Pazour says he then proceeded into the kitchen to make coffee for the group about to arrive, but it seems that the phantom spectral woman was not quite through with him yet. "I came into the kitchen and started making the coffee," he says, "and I was still in shock—not believing what I had just seen. As I was thinking about it, I glanced back toward the parlor and there she was again, this time standing by the archway. She was just there for a split second and then she was gone again.

"A few minutes later," he continues, "I heard talking come from the front of the house, and I thought Amy, my coworker, had arrived. I was pretty anxious for some company at that point so I beat a path to the front door, but there was no one around. As I turned away from the door, I saw her again, this time standing on the staircase. I was totally spooked. I was supposed to go upstairs to open a window, but I wouldn't do it until someone else arrived."

It might be speculated that if there is the spirit of a woman from long ago still walking the hall of the Old County Jail, she seems to have developed a fondness for the young man. "One time, I was in the pantry cleaning out some junk when I felt someone come in behind me and put their arm around my waist. I spun around, but I was alone. I got out of there fast," Pazour remembers.

Another person who claims to have glimpsed the phantom woman is Shirron Soohey, who was a co-manager of the Old Jail Museum. Like Kevin Pazour, her encounter with the feminine specter came when she was preparing the museum for another visit by the Ghost Trackers. "I came in early that evening, and I was walking through the house turning on the lights. When I went to the front of the house, I got the disquieting feeling that someone was watching me. As I walked into the parlor, there was a lady in the dining room. I could not see her clearly—she was a shadowy figure, but I could tell she was dressed in a long dress with a short jacket and a hat. I have to say I got out of there quickly and sat on the front steps till everyone got there."

Ms. Soohey has also witnessed the mysterious swinging of keys on the key rack that others have reported. "We had a professional escape artist come in as a publicity stunt," she remembers. "He was to be locked into one of the cells and then escape. Anyway, the day before, he asked if he could come in to do a dry run—to make sure he could really do it. I took him into the jail and locked him in a cell, and then I went downstairs to the kitchen to wait for him.

"As I sat down I happened to look at the key rack and saw that one of the keys was swinging back and forth slightly. I thought that I must have brushed it as I went by, so I put my hand out and stopped it. Then I went and got a cup of coffee, and when I came back, all the keys were swinging back and forth. I sat there dumbfounded and watched as they swung for five or six minutes and suddenly, they all stopped at once. It was like someone had put out their hand and just stopped them. I checked, and there was no vibration in the wall or floor that could explain it."

Other stories can be culled from both museum guests and staff. One staff member, Kimberly Wiseman, tells of working in the upstairs committee room when she was disturbed by the sound of footsteps coming toward her from the other end of the room. Ignoring the sound, she continued in her efforts until a few moments later when the sound of footsteps began again, approaching her across the cement floor. With her back toward the door, she paused until the steps were within a few inches of her when she turned, expecting to see a fellow worker. To her shock and surprise, she saw the room apparently empty. Thoroughly shocked and more than a little frightened, the young woman ran from the room and searched the building, only to find it vacant.

As has been noted, the tales told of the old jail have generated much interest in the area and have resulted in several newspaper articles and visits from the Indiana Ghost Trackers. However, some of the best work in chronicling the history and ghostly stories of the place has been done by local teacher and documentary film maker, Don Bernacky. Bernacky

photo courtesy of Chris Shultz

Cells at the Old County Jail

and his wife Laura have included the Old Jail Museum as a segment in their entertaining video tape, "Mystic Indiana." During the course of researching and interviewing those involved in the stories, the Bernackys have uncovered a fascinating variety of reported phenomena. However, in a least one instance, they seem to have uncovered more than they had anticipated.

On one occasion while visiting the jail in preparation for filming their documentary, Don remained on the main floor conducting interviews while Laura, acting as cameraperson, explored the upstairs section of the house shooting background footage that could then be edited into the final video tape. Entering the children's bedroom, which is said to be inhabited by a ghostly child, Laura began to film general shots of the room and furniture.

As she did so, she became aware of an odd ticking sound that seemed to come from a glass case against the wall, which housed a collection of antique dolls. Turning her camera toward this case, Laura recorded the sight of one doll, in the center of a row of dolls, moving back and forth seemingly by its own power. Thinking this behavior was the result of a vibration in the building, the case was then examined but no satisfactory answer could be ascertained. The case itself was found to be stable, and even when considerable force was applied to it, no way was found to move just one doll. In the end, the Bernackys and their crew were left wondering if perhaps the very ghosts they had come to chronicle had been seeking to oblige their efforts.

Needless to note, some undoubtedly may choose to debate the reality of the specters said to walk the halls of the museum. For the staff there, however, they are very real. As former intern Kevin Pazour puts it, "Do I think this place is haunted? I would have to say yes. However, if there are ghosts here, I feel like they are a part of the place itself—they have as much right to be here as we do."

The stories told of the Old County Jail Museum continue to be recounted today. Taken alone, each incident might seem merely curious, but placed together they weave a macabre tapestry of ghostly phenomena. As told by staff and visitors to the museum, the tales have become part and parcel of local lore. They are as much a part of this captivating historic structure as the artifacts it houses.

Regrettably, society will probably always have need for jails. Further, as long as people are incarcerated within such places, much of the drama of the dark side of life will be played out there. However, who truly knows but that perhaps as the night draws on and shadows creep within the walls of the Old Jail Museum, some residue of that drama might be replayed. Perhaps, as some believe, a portion of the disquieting history of this place might still reverberate along the corridors and within the darkened cells. They are echoes of a bygone era that still seem to reach out to our present. They are the stuff of legend and folklore and a fascinating part of Indiana ghostlore.

6
THE WISTFUL SPIRITS OF TUCKAWAY

Serene and secluded amidst the busy thrum of city life, the quaint bungalow named Tuckaway sits in a picturesque neighborhood in northern Indianapolis. It is the sort of quaint home that one might pass with little more than a fleeting glance, yet such a passing look would do little justice to one of the most remarkable homes in our state. It is a dwelling that can boast of a history as celebrated and unique as any in the Hoosier state.

The very name of the bungalow, Tuckaway, is an evocative title, conjuring up romantic images from a bygone day. Indeed, the home that bears the name would do nothing to dispel such an impression.

Surrounded by centuries-old trees and tall hedges, Tuckaway has quietly been a feature of the Meridian Park neighborhood for nearly one hundred years. While, on the outside, the California-style bungalow seems only slightly out of place in this heart of the Midwest, it is the history of the structure that places it in the realm of the truly unique. Certainly at first glance, one would never guess that the home has been host to some of the most famous and historic figures of the twentieth century.

The house was built in 1906 in the heart of a glen of trees on what was once believed to be the site of an Indian burial ground. Originally constructed as a modest retreat, the home might well have existed in obscurity except for its purchase in 1910 by George Phillip Meier.

Meier and his wife, Nellie Simmons Meier, were already well known both locally and nationally by the time they acquired their new home. They were two of the most exceptional characters in the annals of Indiana history. By 1901, George Phillip Meier had already begun to rise to the pinnacle of his profession. A grandson of French trappers, Meier had learned the art of being a tailor from his father as a young man. However, not content to simply run a small business in Indianapolis, Meier quickly rose to become a fashion designer of national and, eventually, international renown.

Mr. Meier studied every summer with the House of Worth in Paris, where he and his wife maintained a second home. While in Indiana, he operated from an entire floor of the L.S. Ayers building in downtown Indianapolis. Here forty women were employed full time doing the hand stitching for his creations. Meier also maintained a salon in New York City. His clients were some of the most distinguished and affluent women of the day. A dashing, debonair figure, he was friends with the most glittering stars of the political, artistic and literary worlds. Yet, in terms of personality and personal drive, he was matched by his diminutive but dynamic wife Nellie.

Nellie Simmons Meier, two years his senior, was truly one of the most colorful and vivacious women of her time. While her husband found his reputation in the world of fashion, Nellie soon became famous in a very different realm. As a young woman, Nellie Simmons Meier had become fascinated with the art of chiromancy, or palmistry, an avocation that would take her further than she could ever imagine at the time.

While, today, palm reading conjures up images of gypsy tents and sideshow hucksters, during the late 1800s, at the time of its greatest popularity in the United States, it was seen much more as a science than a mystic art. Nellie Simmons Meier consistently referred to her readings as "scientific palmistry," and argued that through scrupulous examination of her clients' palms, much could be learned about their characters, inclinations and personalities.

Perhaps she was aided in her analysis by an innate empathy and keen instincts about human nature. As Ken Keene, the current owner of Tuckaway, notes, "Her palmistry was her calling card and people flocked to her. I think she probably used her calling in the way a psychologist might later, as a problem solving device. She would see what was in their hand and then hear what was in their heart."

As the *Indianapolis Sunday Star* would later report in a tribute to Mrs. Meier, "Her words could be gently and persuasively revealing to a confused person—suggesting new courage and hope that a greater self-development was possible by honest and determined effort." It was her skill in palmistry would serve as a venue to fame for Nellie Meier. So successful was Mrs. Meier at her craft that it is said that in the 1930s, President Franklin Roosevelt, whose palm she had read several times at the White House, asked her to consult with the FBI in evaluating and establishing the new science of fingerprinting. Later in her career, Nellie was to achieve even greater famc when, in 1937, she wrote a best selling book, *Lion's Paws*, detailing the lives and hands with whom she had become acquainted during her long career.

Whatever the intrinsic value her art (or science) might have had, Nellie Simmons Meier soon became as noteworthy a character in American and international cultural circles as her husband. By the time the pair began looking for a new home in Indianapolis in 1910, they were known as one of the more cultural and affluent couples in Indianapolis. Clearly they could well have built an expansive mansion according to the standards of their time, yet when the Meiers first glimpsed the small home on the north side of Indianapolis, it captured their hearts.

They purchased the house after their first visit and immediately began the process of expanding the home to meet their social and professional tastes. Rather than hire an architect to design their modifications, the Meiers instead chose to rely on their imagination and exquisite artistic vision for their home. A large drawing room was added to the main floor to accommodate their frequent social gatherings as well as additional bedrooms and a sleeping porch on the second floor. A room on the main floor was remodeled specifically as a parlor for Nellie Simmons Meier's palm reading sessions.

By the time their work was done, the Meiers had constructed a masterpiece. The home had been expanded to nine rooms including three bedrooms, two baths, two half baths and a kitchen, which was the domain of the staff cook. Although small by the standards of affluent America, it provided ample living space for Nellie and George Meier as well as a small household staff. Separate living quarters were afforded for a handyman who doubled as a driver for the family.

The interior of the home was reflective of the continental tastes George and Nellie had acquired in their frequent visits to Paris. An elitist linoleum floor was laid in the 1000-foot drawing room, which gleamed with the look of fine leather. Surrounding it were gilded walls and a grand arched, beamed ceiling fifteen feet high, overlooking an oversized fireplace. Furnishings were imported from Europe to create a striking yet warm ambiance.

Despite the ambitious renovations done to the home, the Meiers were still careful to maintain the intimate feel of the house and upon its completion, they bestowed it with the evocative and appropriate title Tuckaway.

In the ensuing decades, the home called Tuckaway became renowned as a social gathering place. Such fame was not without cause, for through the doors of Tuckaway came a parade of the most famous figures of the first half of the twentieth century.

The list of those to visit the home reads as a "Who's Who" of political, artistic and even scientific circles. Eleanor Roosevelt, for whom George Phillip designed two inaugural ball gowns, was a frequent visitor and had her palm read several times there. Walt Disney showed his gratitude for his sessions by sketching cartoons for his hostess. No less a figure than Albert Einstein is reported by a newspaper article of the time to have come to the home as a skeptic with regard to the science of palm reading yet left with "a profound sense of wonder." George Washington Carver was a guest on occasion as was close family friend

James Whitcomb Riley. Amelia Earhart is said to have come to receive a reading from Nellie Simmons Meier prior to taking off on her ill-fated round-the-world flight.

Mrs. Meier's clientele included many of the most famous stars from the arts and entertainment industry as well. Joan Crawford, Mary Pickford and Douglas Fairbanks were all frequent clients. One story holds that Carole Lombard made Tuckaway her last stop on her final visit to Indianapolis on a publicity tour for War Bonds during World War II. According to the tale, Mrs. Meier saw something in her hand that led her to warn Miss Lombard of impending peril, a warning that was apparently disregarded. Ms. Lombard left Tuckaway to go to the Weir Cook Airport in Indianapolis, where she boarded a plane to return to California. Hours later the TWA Skysleeper crashed in Nevada, killing all on board.

The allure of Tuckaway went far beyond Nellie's skill as a palm reader, however. She and her husband also entertained their guests in lavish dinner parties that drew the cream of American society. George Gershwin is said to have played the piano after dinner one evening as did famed pianist Sergci Rachmaninoff, who performed an impromptu

photo courtesy of Mike Pilla

Tuckaway Music Room

concert for the assembled guests in 1941. Isadora Duncan, the famed dancer, tangoed in the drawing room.

Reading the list of all those who were guests in the home, it is hard to imagine this prestigious procession of the rich and famous traveling to a small bungalow in Indianapolis. The fact that they did so is a tribute to both the fame and the gracious hospitality of George Phillip and Nellie Simmons Meier.

At the height of Tuckaway's fame, it was undoubtedly one of the most noted homes in Indiana and perhaps, the United States. It is said that so famous was the house that an international letter addressed simply to "Tuckaway, USA" and would find its way to the home without delay. It was a gathering place for the intellectual, artistic and political luminaries of the day. The legacy of Tuckaway is one of genteel discussion, charming personalities and warm hospitality.

With the passing of George Meier in 1932 followed by that of his wife in 1944, the historic home passed into the possession of their niece, Ruth Austin Peaslee Cannon. Ruth, who had been raised by the Meiers since age fifteen, had gone on to an illustrious career as a dancer. By the 1940s, she had been teaching at a Chicago academy for several years but she willingly returned to Indianapolis to live in Tuckaway. For the next twenty-five years, she made every attempt to maintain the home she loved. However, the years and the declining fortunes of its Meridian Park neighborhood seemed to doom the home to decline.

By the early 1970s, the once illustrious Tuckaway sat empty and forlorn. Boards blocked the windows and weeds choked the once splendid yard. It was then that the home was discovered by Ken Keene.

"I had always wanted to own an old house," Ken now explains. "I was working in downtown Indianapolis and I knew and loved the Meridian Park neighborhood. One day, I came down here on my lunch hour, pushed my way through the weeds and the overgrown shrubbery and I looked at this boarded-up house."

To say that Mr. Keene's reaction was love at first sight would be an understatement. "I had an epiphany, like I have never had in my life. I lost all track of time and didn't even go back to my office after my lunch hour was done. About midnight, I finally left the place. I went home, called up some friends at 3:00 A.M. and told them I had found my house."

While there was no "For Sale" sign in the front yard (Mr. Keene would later discover that Mrs. Cannon could not bear the thought of placing such a sign in front of her beloved home), through Ruth's lawyer Ken found that the house was indeed for sale. Moreover, he was delighted to discover that the house and its contents could be purchased for just $12,500.

"The house was in bad repair, the furniture was gone and the neighborhood, at that point, was pretty bad, but I just knew I had to own this house," Mr. Keene remembers. "At this point I knew nothing of its history or of the Meiers and who they were, but I somehow knew that I was destined to own it."

Part of this revelation came when Ken met Ruth Cannon, with whom he felt an instant connection. As he grew to know Mrs. Cannon, he began to learn something of the history of the home he was now purchasing. A second and yet more surprising discovery came when Mr. Keene began to open boxes stored in the basement.

"I started opening these boxes and suddenly, I found myself looking at all these hand prints of stars and some incredibly famous people. I started to pull out literally hundreds of pictures, all autographed to Nellie Simmons Meier. I felt like I had found a treasure trove."

As Ken took possession of the home and continued to piece together the history of the house and those who had lived there, a new passion rose in his heart: to return Tuckaway to its former splendor. "I had pictures of the interior of the home but I have never tried to find exact copies of any one piece," he recounts. "Instead, I have just tried to recreate the general look of the place. I was obsessive—I came to realize that if I did not put it together the way it was, I had to do it over and over until I got it right."

Visiting the home today, it is readily apparent that Mr. Keene's "obsession" has resulted in one of the most striking and authentically restored homes in the United States. As *American Bungalow* magazine recently noted in a feature article on Tuckaway, "Looking at Tuckaway today, it's hard to tell that George and Nellie Meier ever left the place." Ken Keene has taken great care to ensure that no vestige of modern style or accents can be seen. Every detail of the house, from the vintage furniture to the flooring and draperies, has been carefully chosen to sweep the visitor back to a more refined, genteel era.

This restoration has been done with obvious love and care. Gilded walls are resplendent and beautiful and the woodwork seems to glow in the firelight. The vintage furniture is at once graceful and yet comfortable, contributing to the warmth and charm that pervades the home.

Perhaps some of the most striking accents to the home are the many autographed photos lining the walls, each documenting a famous life linked to its history. Every piece of this fascinating collection is personally autographed, most with an inscription to Nellie Meier. A photo of Joan Crawford bears the sentiment, "With my profound gratitude." Across a picture of George Gershwin is the neatly lettered dedication, "In appreciation for your gifts." Beneath a hand-drawn cartoon of Mickey Mouse, one reads the message, "Keep it, my dear, it might be worth something some day, because I drew it myself. Walt."

To visit the bungalow of Tuckaway is to be caught up in the mesmerizing ambiance of the place. During the daylight hours, the sun casts its light through the tall oaks outside, dappling the interior of the house in gentle light. As evening comes and darkness draws close, the warm light of a generous fire in the grate casts shadows across the gold walls and rich furnishings. From somewhere in the house, an antique melody floats gently through the rooms like the scent of fine perfume. The venerable old home creaks quietly, as though softly sighing. It is in moments such as these that wistful spirits are said to walk the gilded halls of Tuckaway once more.

"The first hint of ghosts in the house came long before my time, when the Meiers were still living here," Mr. Keene relates. "I learned from a great niece of the Meiers that their dogs would sometimes walk over to empty chairs, wag their tails and sit as though they were watching something or someone that no one else could see."

Interestingly, Ken notes that this odd behavior has been mimicked by several dogs that he has had over the years. However, in the scope of peculiar occurrences reported at Tuckaway, these canine incidents seem simply the tip of the spectral iceberg.

Mr. Keene relates that while he had no knowledge of any ghostly presence when he purchased the home and began his work of restoration, he soon began to hear reports that caught his attention. "For many years," he describes, "I supplemented my income by renting out rooms to students from Indiana University/Purdue University Indianapolis. Eventually, they began telling me stories of some of the things that happened to them in the house. What strikes me is that many of them told the same stories over a thirty-year period. Their stories matched and the people never met."

According to Keene, more than a few of his guests reported waking from their sleep to see spectral faces suspended over their bed, peering down at them genially. One of the faces, that of a woman, is frequently said to have smiled, winked and then vanished. "As they described the faces, they sounded like a good description of George and Nellie Meier. Maybe they were just checking in on who was staying in their home."

Considering the tales told by Ken Keene, as well as by many of the visitors to Tuckaway over the years, it seems that the Meiers have kept a lively interest in their beloved bungalow, despite their departure from the physical realm. Their presence has been seen, heard and felt for many years throughout the house.

"They have been seen many times at my costume parties," he remarks, "which I have regularly held over the years. I think that they like costume parties because they know they will blend in." As Mr. Keene now explains, it has been his custom over the last thirty years to host costume parties both as social gatherings and as charity events for local community groups. On several of these occasions, he seems to have entertained more guests than he anticipated at the time.

"One particular evening I will never forget," Ken continues, warming to his story. "I had a good friend who had moved from Indianapolis to California to be involved in the movie industry. A couple of times,

photo courtesy of Mike Pilla

Tuckaway Dining Room

she came back to visit and would stay with me for a week or so. When she would come back she always wanted to have a costume party with a twenties theme. So, she would call down to Butler University where she had connections with the drama department and arrange to borrow some of their vintage costumes. Then, she would ask them to round up some students, dress them up and have them come to the party. The consequence was that I was the host of a party where I didn't know most of my guests, but of course, I never minded."

It was at one of those fateful parties that a young guest had an inexplicable encounter with the friendly spirits of Tuckaway.

"It was in the summertime," Ken remembers, "and the party was getting going. Everyone was dressed in costumes from the twenties and we were having a great time. A student at the piano was playing 'Over There,' and everyone was gathered around singing. I was carrying a big tray of punch down the hallway when two girls in their early twenties came in. One of them asked me if this was my house. She asked if she could look around, and I told her that they could go anywhere. Then, on impulse, I told her not to miss the upstairs sleeping porch. Then I went on down the hall into the parlor and she went upstairs to look around."

Mr. Keene remembers that as he served his guests and stood with them around the piano, suddenly their congenial sounds were interrupted by a more shocking noise. "A scream erupted from upstairs," he describes, "that Alfred Hitchcock could not have produced. It was followed a moment later by the thumps of feet pounding down the stairs. The girl bolted down the stairs, flew out the door and barreled into the street.

"The music immediately stopped, and we all kind of stared wide-eyed at one another. The girl she had come with hurried after her, and we went to the front porch and watched as they stopped by the car and had an obviously heated discussion. Then, after a minute, the girl who had been upstairs got into her car and burned rubber down the street.

"After a minute," Mr. Keene continues, "the friend came walking back to the house, visibly upset. As she got back to the porch, I went out to meet her, but before I could say anything, she looked at me and asked, 'My friend said you sent her up to the sleeping porch—is that right?' I responded, 'Yes, so what?' Then she told me what had happened."

According to the story, her friend had gone upstairs to take a look around. As she toured the second floor, she ventured onto the shuttered sleeping porch. As she stood on the porch enjoying the view of the backyard, she became aware of a sense that she was not alone.

Turning to glance at the far end of the porch, she was surprised to see an elderly couple standing there, also apparently enjoying the warmth of the summer evening. As she described the pair to her friend, it seemed obvious they were dressed for the party, for they wore costumes dating from the 1920s. The man wore a white woolen suit with a white straw hat and a well groomed mustache. His companion was a plump woman nearly a foot shorter than he with a pleasant round face.

Overcoming her shock, since she had assumed herself alone on the porch, the young woman quickly conjectured the pair to be her host's grandparents and decided it only polite to greet them. Smiling, she turned and approached the couple and introduced herself, extending her hand in greeting. As she later related, the couple turned toward her, smiled warmly and then simply disappeared. It was this unorthodox departure that precipitated her scream and hasty exit from the home.

Significantly, as Ken Keene heard the story that night standing on his front porch, he realized that, once again, the description of the elderly couple fit well with that of George Phillip and Nellie Simmons Meier. As he now muses, perhaps it is natural that the former owners of the home would turn out to enjoy the festivities.

Nor is this the only instance of an unexpected guest making an appearance at one of Keene's parties. Another incident happened at a Halloween party that occurred in the early 1980s. As Ken now remembers the occasion, "It was early in the evening, about half an hour before the guests were to arrive, when there was a knock at the door. It was a man who I did not recognize and who was without a costume. He explained that he was an architect from out of town who had met a lady name Kitty, who was to be my hostess that night, at a business meeting that day. She had invited him to drop by the party that night and he had agreed. He was embarrassed, however, because he had arrived early and without a costume, but I invited him in.

"He said that he was fascinated with the architecture of the place," Ken continues, "and asked if he could look around. I told him that was fine and asked him if he would go to the basement and check on some candles I had set up there for a Halloween maze for the guests. He agreed and wandered off."

A short time later, as Ken was greeting his guests, the man appeared at his elbow and asked if he could speak to him. "I was a little busy right then, between the guests arriving and the trick or treaters coming to the door, but before I could put him off, he asked, 'By any chance is this house haunted?' That got my attention, and I asked him to come with me to the library. When we got there, I asked him what had happened."

In a quiet and sincere tone, the man told his host that he had wandered downstairs and looked around a bit. He had found the maze and gone through, checking to make sure the candles were all safe as he had been asked. When he came out of the maze, he saw a stunning young woman with long brown hair and large eyes attired in a beautiful dress from the early 1900s walking toward him from a corner of the basement. Thinking that she was a costumed guest, the man greeted her and commented, "That's a beautiful costume you are wearing." Smiling, the young woman replied, "Thank you. My uncle designed it for me." "Aren't you chilly on this cool October night?" the man continued. "Oh, no!" answered the coy young woman, who then turned, winked and simply vanished.

"When the man finished telling me what happened," Ken concludes, "I pointed to a picture of Ruth Cannon, the Meier's niece who had sold me the house. I asked, 'Did she look anything like this?' and he kind of gasped, 'That's her!' I was shocked but not all that surprised. Ruth had been raised by the Meiers and had only worn dresses designed by George Phillip Meier." Needless to note, Ruth Cannon had passed away a number of years before this incident.

It seems that more than a few people over the years have reported catching a glimpse of one of the former owners in the home. Mr. Keene notes that his father, a former brigadier general, reported seeing George Phillip Meier several times standing at the top of the stairs staring serenely down at him as he entered the house. Others, too, have reported his presence there.

One young man who recently stayed at Tuckaway reported walking by the master bedroom one morning and glancing in to see a woman sleeping in the bed. He describes her as being in her forties with dark, curly hair. According to Mr. Keene, this description fits Ruth Cannon, who used that bedroom after the death of her aunt and uncle.

Interestingly, Ken Keene says that he has never directly seen any of the ghosts said to inhabit his home, although he did once wake from a fitful sleep to see what he describes as a "milky white haze" floating over his bed. After a few moments, he recalls, the foggy mist disappeared, seeming to slowly dissipate into the ambient air. However, this is not his only encounter with the spirits.

He says that he has routinely heard inexplicable things in the home. "I frequently hear the sound of someone walking up to the front porch, opening the mailbox and letting it shut with a bang as though checking for mail." Invariably, when Ken peers out the window, the porch is empty. He also reports hearing the sound of flute music floating through the house late at night. He describes it as a sad, beautiful, haunting sound.

Others, too, have frequently reported hearing strange sounds in Tuckaway. "It usually occurs when I am out of town and I have people house-sitting for me. They tell me that late at night, they will hear the faint sound of a piano playing as well as muffled conversation and the clink of cocktail glasses. Some have even said that when they stand at the top of the stairs, they can see vague shadows moving on the main floor, even though the house is empty except for them." Perhaps they are witness to a social gathering of otherworldly guests assembling once more for good conversation and genial "spirits."

One of the more bizarre encounters told to Ken came several years ago by a young woman named Beth, who had once rented a room at Tuckaway. "Beth had rented a room from me in about 1980 and then moved out of town. A few years later she moved back to Indianapolis and asked if she could rent a room again," he explains. "Her first night back in the house, we were sitting talking and she said to me, 'Did I ever tell you about the first night that I spent here?' When I told her she hadn't, she replied, 'I guess I never thought that you'd believe it.' So I coaxed the story out of her.

photo courtesy of Mike Pilla

Tuckaway Living Room

"She revealed that the very first night she moved into this house she had a dream, or at least she thought it was a dream, " Ken recounts. "She told me that in this dream, all the sheets, even the ones underneath her body, were being pulled off. As though that was not weird enough, the sheets began to float around the room, twisting and billowing into shapes—almost dancing around and around the room. Then, as she lay there watching this bizarre show, she looked up at the ceiling and saw a woman's face smiling down at her. To her utter amazement, she watched the face smile and wink and then everything went black. I said, 'So you dreamed all of this?' She answered, 'I thought so, but when I woke up that morning, I was lying on the bare mattress and the bedclothes were draped all around the room!'"

The vast majority of encounters at Tuckaway are of a pleasant, almost playful nature. However, in at least one instance the phenomena seem to have taken on a more ominous and frightening tone.

According to Keene, the story in question began late one winter afternoon in January of 1978. "I remember the day specifically because it was the beginning of one of the worst blizzards we ever had. The temperature dropped fast, the winds picked up and snow started blowing in." As Ken now recalls, early that afternoon, as the snow began falling, two young men arrived at his door begging lodging for the night. "I knew one of the guys, and he told me that they had just arrived back in Indianapolis from Florida and they had no money and no place to stay. He remembered that I had extra bedrooms and sometimes let them out. I told them they could come in and spend the night, especially since the weather was pretty bad and I didn't want to leave them in the street."

Ken goes on to mention that as the evening grew closer, he realized that he was not adequately provisioned for guests and he decided to make a quick trip to a grocery store before the weather made traveling completely impossible. Taking one of the young men with him, Ken ventured out into the wind and snow. After purchasing their supplies, the pair had returned to within a block of Tuckaway when they caught sight of a figure walking through the snow away from the home.

"I looked and even through the blowing snow, I could see that it was the young man we had left at the house," Ken says. "He seemed to be in a hurry going somewhere, but he wasn't going to get far in that weather, so I pulled over and asked him to get into the car. It took some convincing to get him into the car and even more to get him to go back to Tuckaway. He was shaking from more than the cold and even crying, and all he would say was, 'You have that house rigged!' I had no idea what he was talking about, but we eventually got him back in the house and warmed up. Then I asked him what he was doing out in the snow.

"He started shaking all over again and told me that after we left, he had started walking through the house, kind of looking around. He said that when he got to the hall where I have all the pictures hanging, suddenly all the pictures starting swinging back and forth in unison. Each of those pictures is on a hanger nailed into the wall and I can tell you they are all very, very secure. In the entire time I have lived here, I have never known one to move, much less all of them at once and yet, he swore that's what happened. At that exact moment, all the lights in the hall, which are on dimmers, suddenly started going up and down on their own. He got so scared he grabbed his coat and ran out into the snow."

As strange as this incident may seem, perhaps the sprits of Tuckaway were just getting warmed up that evening. As Ken now remembers, after the young man calmed somewhat, he decided to retire for the night. However, when Ken rose the next morning, he found that the young man was gone. Gravely concerned, the young man's friend began making phone calls to mutual friends in an effort to discover his whereabouts.

Two days later, they located the young man in another home far from Tuckaway. He admitted leaving Tuckaway in the middle of the night and walking more than ten miles through a blizzard and numbing temperatures to the house of a family friend, where he broke a window to gain entrance. When asked what would drive him to such extreme measures, the young man swore that after going to bed, he had been awakened in the early hours of the morning by an odd feeling. Sitting up abruptly, he knocked his head on the ceiling before looking down to find the bed floating several feet from the floor. Horrified, he rolled off the bed, collapsed onto the floor below and ran from the home.

While such a story might seem impossible on its surface, Mr. Keene notes that something had driven the young man from a warm home into a blizzard that night and he steadfastly refused to ever return to Tuckaway. Further, Ken later discovered that the young man in question had a criminal record, including charges of theft, and he surmises that perhaps Nellie or George Phillip Meier did not approve of his presence in the home. If this is the case, then they must be credited with a novel and rather striking way to rid themselves of an unwanted houseguest.

Despite this rather macabre episode, on the whole, the ghosts of Tuckaway seem to be an agreeable, genial lot. One might wonder if the specters are those of the legion of the rich and famous who came through the doors of this lovely home nearly a century ago. Perhaps, as Ken Keene believes, they are the spirits of the Meier family, returning to watch over the home in which they had so much happiness. If this is the case, then the Meiers seem to approve of their beloved home being restored to its former beauty. "I feel loved and protected here," Ken Keene expresses, a smile warming his face. "It is not a horrific place at all. This is my home and I love it."

There is much to love in this gracious, elegant dwelling, now painstakingly returned to the beauty it once enjoyed. From a fascinating history to a myriad of former guests that includes some of the most noted personalities of the last century, it is one of the most singular homes in our state. Moreover, if the tales whispered are to be believed, there is much of Tuckaway that goes beyond even its striking history and beauty. For, as evening surrounds the home in its dark embrace, it is said that the otherworldly visitors walk, or dance, its gilded halls once more.

Far from the frightful specters of popular media, these apparitions are said to be gentle spirits returning to protect their beloved home or perhaps simply relive a happy memory from a day and age long gone. In any case, they, like the home they inhabit, are a curious, intriguing and extraordinary part of our state history and a fascinating part of Hoosier ghostlore.

7
A GHOST ON THE BEAT

Your basic street cop seems like a hard bitten, cynical, jaded individual. We are the last line of defense between society and those who would do it harm. Solitary, except to those within his or her own profession, reticent to share or trust, the street cop stands utterly grounded in a reality most people would rather ignore. Yet, deep within, there is a core of nobility in the best of us, a sense of duty and honor that neither experience nor cynicism can quite erase. Lurking deep inside the street fighting warrior there still exists the heart of the knight.

—John Camphern, ***Blue Reflections***

This is, perhaps, an apt description of the persona of those in police work. Police, from our rural sheriff departments to big-city police forces, are perhaps some of the most grounded, realistic individuals in our society. By nature and by training, the men and women who wear a badge deal with reality every day. Their stock and trade is to handle the immediacies of life. Often overworked, underpaid and nearly always underappreciated by the public, there is little in their day-to-day lives that allows for the fanciful, the abstract, or the imaginative.

It would seem natural that police officers in general would be poor candidates to experience or relate ghostly happenings. One might assume that within the ranks of police work, mention of the supernatural would bring only scoffs.

However, this does not seem to be the case. Although naturally reticent to talk about such beliefs or experiences, when many police do talk about the paranormal, strange and seemingly inexplicable tales are often told.

As Carl Madison,* a retired police officer from Elkhart reflects, "Of course, it is hard to get police to talk about things like that. No one but a raw rookie is going to get on the police radio and announce he is chasing down a ghost. But, if you get the guys talking around the squad room drinking coffee, some weird experiences start to come out, especially from the veterans. If you think about it, we are called into some pretty strange places, at odd hours of the day and night. Sometimes we experience things that we just cannot explain. Sometimes it is just an unbearable sense of presence—you are in some place that's deserted, and you just know that you're not alone, and that whatever else is there with you is not exactly human. At those times it is easier to ignore what may be going on than to investigate it. If my law isn't broken—if I can't put handcuffs on whatever is there, then it is easier to walk away."

Officer Madison knows whereof he speaks, for in his twenty years in the department he encountered several incidents that seemed, at the time, to be more than a little odd.

Once such occurrence took place on a bitterly cold night in the winter of 1977, when Madison was on patrol on the outskirts of Elkhart. "It was January, with a snow blowing in and a wind chill of about 10 below. The kind of a night when you hope that next to nothing happens so that you can stay warm in your squad car," he now recalls.

"I seem to recall that we had just a couple of calls that night—typical incidents for the weather. A couple of accidents, or cars gone down into the ditch—this is the kind of stuff you get on a winter night. Then, about 11:30 or so I got a call to go out and check an abandoned warehouse a few miles from my location. Someone had driven by and seen lights in the place. I thought, 'Great—just what I need on a night like this—to go into a cold, drafty building and have to chase out some poor homeless guy who just wants to get out of the snow,' but, of course, that goes with the job."

As Officer Madison drove into the parking lot and left his patrol car, he decided to first do a perimeter check of the building, to see if there were any obvious signs of a break-in. "To the rear of the building I found a door that at some point had been pried open—how long ago I could not tell, but it looked like it had been jimmied." Returning to his car, Officer Madison radioed the station requesting backup. "I was not anticipating any trouble, but if there was some chasing to be done, I wanted some help. Besides, that was our standard procedure."

Within a few minutes, his call was answered by another Elkhart patrol as well as a county sheriff's deputy that was in the area. "I told my guy to come inside with me, while the county guy stayed outside to watch the door, to catch anyone that might leave the building in a hurry. Then, as quietly as we could, we entered the building."

Walking slowly through the office area of the long deserted warehouse, the two officers quietly made their way by the light of their flashlights through the dust and debris strewn along the floors. Finding nothing and no one, they proceeded toward the cavernous warehouse itself.

"We got to the door leading into the warehouse section, and as I went to grab the handle my buddy stopped my hand and pointed at the window. The door had a small frosted glass window, but you could see a yellowish light, like a candle or a fire faintly shining from the other side. I nodded to him, now completely convinced that we had kids or more probably a homeless person trying to get in out of the cold. But to be on the safe side I put one hand on my service revolver and threw open the door, loudly announcing myself as a police officer."

However, upon entering the warehouse the two officers found it dark and empty, with no apparent source for the light they had seen reflecting through the window a moment before. Telling his partner to check the far door, Officer Madison began searching the main area of the warehouse for anyone who might be hiding there.

"It was a big room, and dark, but it was also totally empty, except for a couple of big pieces of machinery along the back wall. There was no good place for a person to hide, and I was shining my light everywhere. There was simply no one there. I had about decided that the perpetrator had gotten out the rear door into the back hallway when suddenly I heard one heck of a crash from the far wall. I jumped about a foot, and almost automatically, I pulled my revolver."

Briskly walking in the direction of the noise, Officer Madison found that a large metal container, which might have once contained tools, had fallen from a shelf and onto the floor. While this explained the source of the noise, he still was at a loss to explain how it had come to fall in the first place.

"That wall had just a couple of machines set up against it, with no place to hide. It was just the matter of a split second between the time I heard the bang and when I shone my flashlight there, and there was no time for anyone to run."

Still, as Officer Madison carefully searched the area, he found no trace of anyone. Further, noting the thick dust that covered the floor, he saw no trace of footsteps. "I looked down and could not figure it out. The metal box probably weighed ten pounds, and while it was a drafty place there was sure not enough wind in that room to knock over a box that size. I was about to shrug it off when I heard the other officer calling me from the far side of the room."

Running to his fellow officer, he found the man pointing down a long hall that led from the warehouse. Excitement tingeing his voice, the officer told Madison that he had been searching that area when he heard the crash from the opposite side of the room. Turning in that direction, he had caught sight of something in the hall in his peripheral vision. As he looked toward the open doorway leading to the hall, he had seen a light proceeding down the hall away from the warehouse.

"I said to the guy 'Great, I don't know how he got out, but we have got this guy now. His flashlight is going to give him away,' but before I could go to the door he stopped me and told me that he had not seen the light of a flashlight. Instead, he said that he had seen a perfect ball of light, and it seemed to be floating down the hallway. I told him 'You're nuts—it must be a trick of the light. Lights don't float, they get carried, and we are going to catch the guy who is carrying it.' But he swore that he had seen it—an orb of light about three feet off the ground sort of leisurely floating down the hall."

Adrenalin now jolting their senses, the pair entered the hallway and proceeded toward the office at the far end. As they entered the hallway, they were greeted only by darkness. However, as they made their way toward the office at the end of the hall, Madison says that he could vaguely begin to see a faint light shining from the office on the other side. "It was an orangish, reddish light—I thought maybe from a candle or small fire. Now I was as ticked off as I was excited, and I was not in a mood to play games. I got to the end of the hall and kicked the door open as hard as I could and yelled 'Police!' What happened next I could not believe."

With a slight stiltedness creeping into his speech, Carl Madison relates that as he kicked open the door, he and his fellow officer were suddenly buffeted by a blast of cold, angry wind. "This was no breeze," he now recalls, "it was a sudden, gale-force wind. It was strong enough that it nearly knocked me over, and then it was just gone. It blew past me like a tsunami of cold wind—colder than even the temperature of the building to begin with, and then it was still again. I looked at the other cop and said 'What the heck was that?'"

Pausing just long enough to ascertain that the room before them was empty, the pair moved back toward the warehouse, noting that theirs were the only footprints left in the dust on the floor. Finding the warehouse section still vacant, the pair left the building and found their colleague waiting for them by the back door.

"I was going to ask the county guy if he had seen anyone, but before I could, he asked me 'Did you catch him?' Not quite sure how to explain what had happened in the building I just said 'No, it's empty.' When I said that this weird look came over the officer's face and he said 'Bull! How about whoever was running around with that yellow ball!'"

The deputy then went on to excitedly explain how, after watching his fellow officers enter the building he had seen several streaks of light moving at a high rate of speed though the windows of the loading dock door. Thinking them to be flashlights, and wondering if they were pursuing someone through the building, he had walked over to peer through the windows. He stated that through the frost of the window he could see into the loading area, where he observed the same ball of light that had been seen inside the hallway. He described it as perfectly round, and about three inches in diameter, giving off a soft, yellowish incandescence. After a few moments, the light seemed to circle the room and then simply went out.

"This young guy was all hyped up for going back into the building, but I had had enough for one night. I told him to get back on the road and forget about the whole thing. I assured him, and I believe today, that there was no living person in that building," Madison relates.

Together, Madison and his fellow officer returned to their station to discuss what had occurred. Clearly, neither could come up with a rational explanation for the glowing balls of light, nor the strange wind that had whipped past them in the hall. Perhaps wisely, the two decided not to file an official report on what they had experienced.

This could well have put an end to the story, except for a final note that came some months later, when the two policemen were together with a group of officers in the squad room of the station.

"A bunch of us were sitting around after the shift drinking coffee and passing some stories back and forth," Madison remembers, "when the guy who had been with me that night looked at me and said 'What about what happened to us at the warehouse that night?'

"I really did not want to tell the story, but as soon as he said that an old veteran on the force looked at me and said 'What warehouse was that?' Somewhat reluctantly, I told him the location, and before I could go any further he looked at me very directly and said, 'You mean you've been on the force this long and you don't know not to go into that place after dark? We've been getting reports on that warehouse for years and most of us just ignore them—that place is supposed to be haunted by a workman who was crushed to death when some machinery toppled over on him thirty years ago!' And with that," Madison concludes, "I let the story drop. Twenty years on the force has taught me that some things are best left alone."

Perhaps, as Officer Madison surmises, some things are better left alone. However, in other cases, leaving well enough alone is not an option, as eerie events reach out to touch the lives of the officers. In at least one case, this phrase seems to be literally applicable.

Mike Grill is a former Allen County sheriff's deputy, who served for ten years before taking a job in the private sector. During his time on the force, Grill relates dealing with everything from drug arrests to grisly accidents, yet nothing prepared him for an event that occurred in 2001 in a seemingly prosaic home in the suburbs of Fort Wayne.

As Grill now remembers, it was while on patrol one warm spring evening that he received a call on his police radio requesting an officer to check on noises at a home in a quiet residential district nearby. While the home was technically in the city precincts of Fort Wayne, it was customary for available county deputies to assist as backup for city police, so he radioed in that he would respond. Arriving at the house, he found a Fort Wayne city policeman sitting in his squad car looking grim.

He walked up to the unit and talked to the officer, who he knew slightly, asking him what the problem was. Looking at Officer Grill somberly, the officer said that he was not sure, but that it was a house the Fort Wayne Police Department had received numerous calls on over the last year. He explained that the first call they had received was when the son of the owners was found dead of suicide in an upstairs bedroom. The young man, apparently under the influence of narcotics, had hung himself, and ever since that time his grief-stricken parents had periodically called in to report strange noises or objects moving in the house.

"I looked at the officer like he was crazy," Mike recalls, "and he told me not to get spooked—they had never found anything and the police thought is was simply a case of parents having trouble coping with the death of their son, and imagination doing the rest. We knocked on the door, and an elderly woman answered, obviously distraught. She asked us in and told us that all evening they had been hearing knocking in an upstairs bedroom. The other officer shot me a look that told me it was probably the room where the boy hung himself."

While Grill denies being "spooked" (in his words) by this eerie and somewhat macabre call, he does admit feeling a bit apprehensive about dealing with parents who, in their grief, might have become emotionally unstable. However, the officers calmly assured the woman and her husband that they would thoroughly investigate upstairs, and would report anything they found to the couple. Then, asking the elderly parents to stay in the downstairs living room, the officers ascended the main stairs toward the upstairs hallway.

"I was telling myself that this was all routine as I was walking up the stairs, but when we got to the landing at the top I heard what sounded like a crash coming from behind a door at the end of the hall. I shot the other cop a look and said, 'I thought you said this was just in their heads!' and he said, 'Yea, that's what I thought too.'"

Both of their nerves a bit on edge, the pair walked down the hallway toward the closed door. "It is hard to describe," Grill now says, "but it seemed like it took us an eternity to walk to the end of that hall. In my mind I was telling myself that there was someone behind that door, or that something had just fallen naturally, but I can tell you that it simply felt like there was someone else in the upstairs with us. As a policeman, you tend to develop a sense for when you are not alone, and maybe it was just the nerves, but I sure felt a sense of presence with us that night. The air was thick with the feeling of someone, or something there."

As they walked toward the door, Grill remembers hearing at least one more muffled thump coming from the bedroom, followed by an ominous silence. "We paused at the door and the city guy looked at me, like he was waiting for me to do something, but I leaned over and whispered 'This is your call—you go in first!'"

Grill recalls that before opening the door he saw his fellow officer reach down and undo the safety latch on the holster holding his service revolver. Then, a bit nervously, the officer called out, "Police officer—we're coming in!"

Flinging open the door, the pair sprang into the room, only to find it dark and apparently vacant. Grill found a light switch and turned it on, but nothing was amiss. Carefully, the officers searched the room for anyone hiding, or any sign of what might have fallen to make the loud thumps they had heard from the hallway, but found no possible source.

The room was empty, but Grill recalls feeling strongly that it was not vacant. "It is hard to describe, without sounding crazy, but the sense of presence was nearly overpowering in that room. I'm no psychic, and I certainly don't feel ghosts around me, but I can tell you for a fact that everything inside of me wanted to get out of that room. Something was there, and I don't think it wanted us around. The other cop must have felt it too, because pretty quickly he turned to me and said, 'That's it—let's get downstairs.'"

Relieved to be leaving the room, the officers left, shutting the door, and began to walk down the hallway toward the stairs. According to his report, however, Officer Grill's relief was premature and short-lived.

"Now I know this sound really nuts," he says, "but I hadn't taken three steps down that hall when something hit me, and hit me hard. I'm a big guy, about six-foot-three, and back then I probably weighed in at 240, but whatever it was hit me so hard it nearly lifted me off my feet and threw me at least four feet into a wall. It was not like hands pushing you or anything—it was just this sudden force, and it was strong. I played defensive line in football all through high school, and I had never felt anything hit me that hard."

Crashing into the wall with tremendous force, Grill jumped to his feet, his service revolver in hand. "I was looking for whatever son of a [expletive deleted] had just hit me, but when I got to my feet the other officer, who was a few feet ahead, was just standing there staring at me. I managed to gasp, 'What was that—who just crashed into me?' but he swore that there was no one in the hall. His back had been turned and when he heard the crash of me hitting the wall he turned just in time to see me staggering to my feet looking for someone to shoot."

Together the two did a quick search of the other rooms in the upstairs section of the house, finding them vacant. "When we were done," Grill says today, "the other officer looked at me and said, 'So, what do you suppose we should tell the folks downstairs?' I rubbed my shoulder, which was pretty sore from hitting that wall, and said, 'You tell them anything you want. This isn't my jurisdiction and I'm going back to the office.' Then I left. Ordinarily I wouldn't have gone anywhere till the investigation was completed, but I was pretty well shook up, I can tell you. I don't know what that poor cop told those folks, but there was a bruise on my shoulder and back for at least a week afterward. It was the strangest thing I have ever encountered, and not one I care to repeat."

As violent and inexplicable as Officer Grill's story might be, it is not the only eerie tale told by policemen and women from our state. One of the oddest tales is one that has been handed down for twenty years through select members of the Indianapolis Police Department. Today it is told by Theresa Scherzinger,* whose father Robert was on the Indianapolis police force for more than thirty years.

"My dad was an old-time cop," she now recalls with obvious fondness. "He was a rough and tumble man, with grit down to the bottom of his soul. He was also the least imaginative person you could imagine—what was real was real to my dad, and that was all there was to it, which makes the story he told us of the ghost car doubly intriguing."

As Theresa now recalls, her father never spoke much about his job to her or her three brothers, preferring to protect them from the knowledge of the dangers of his profession.

"My dad never wanted to worry us kids, so he rarely talked about the stuff that happened on the street. However, once in a great while, particularly at family gatherings when he had a beer or two in him, he would open up and some really interesting stories came out."

One such occasion occurred at a family dinner in late October in the late eighties, shortly after his retirement from the force. Sitting in the living room with his extended family, the subject of Halloween came up and hence the subject of ghosts. One family member speculated that the old house in which Theresa and her family lived might be haunted, but her father quickly dismissed the idea.

"But then," Theresa notes, "I can still remember that my dad looked down for a second, like he was thinking of something, and then put his beer on the table. This usually meant that he was going to say something serious. He looked at us gathered around and said, 'I don't know about ghosts, but I sure as heck did see one thing in my time on the force that shook me up pretty good. And it wasn't any ghost—not exactly. It was a ghost car.'"

Intrigued, his children leaned close as Robert slowly warmed to his tale. "My dad started by saying that it happened on the far south side of Indianapolis, in an area that a long time ago was called Dragster Hallow. Today it is all built up with businesses and shopping malls, but when I was a kid it was still pretty rural. There was a straightaway on the road there that went for a couple of miles, and I guess in the fifties kids used to go out there and drag race their cars. My dad said that over the years there were more than a couple of bad crashes out there as a result of those races, and some kids had been killed."

Robert went on to relate that one night about 1975 he was on patrol in the area of Dragster Hallow. "Dad said that it was a Friday night in the fall," Theresa says, "prime time for drag racing, and so about midnight he decided to drive out to Dragster Hallow to see if any kids were there. When he got to that stretch of road he found no one there—the road was vacant. Understand that the road is perfectly straight for a couple of miles, so you can see any headlight in front or behind for a long ways, and Dad said there was no one on the road."

Relieved to find to find no activity in the area, Robert reported that he drove down the straightaway for about half a mile when suddenly his reverie was disturbed in an uncanny way.

"Dad very seriously told us that he had driven a short distance when a car suddenly appeared behind him and whipped past him like he was standing still. Dad said he was doing about fifty and this guy left him in the dirt. Later, when he had time to think about it, he said he was shocked, because he had not seen headlights coming up behind him, but at the time he didn't think, he just hit his lights and sirens and took off after the guy."

According to the tale Officer Scherzinger told his children, he sped through the night after the mysterious vehicle, which did not even slow down in response to his lights and siren. Pressing his accelerator till he was driving nearly seventy miles an hour, he did draw close enough to get a closer look at the car he was chasing.

"My father was an aficionado of cars," Theresa reflects. "He could name the year and make of any car at a glance, and swore to us that when he got close enough to look at that car, it was a '55 Chevy. He said it looked like it had just rolled off the showroom—a deep midnight blue with the chrome from the bumper shining back from his headlights."

Feverishly, Officer Scherzinger radioed in his location and asked for assistance. No matter how fast he drove, the car ahead stayed tantalizingly out of reach, never allowing him to approach too closely.

"Dad said that it was like the guy in the car was playing cat and mouse with him. He would let him get close and then accelerate out ahead. At this point Dad did not know if the driver was a drunk or some kid out hot-rodding, but Dad was starting to get mad, and he vowed to himself that someone was going to spend the night in jail when he did catch up. Then, he said, things got really weird."

As Theresa tells the story, suddenly the car accelerated with great velocity and shot out ahead of her father's patrol cruiser, which was doing at least seventy-five miles per hour. Then, unexpectedly, slowed slightly and turned up a side lane.

"My father said when he saw the car take the turn he knew in his gut that there was something very strange going on, because it had barely slowed down to make the turn. He estimated that the car was doing at least seventy-five when it made the turn, but he swore that it turned like it was on rails—the tires did not even slide."

For his part, Officer Scherzinger had to slam on his breaks, fishtailing into the curve in order to safely maneuver around the sharp corner. Narrowly avoiding the ditch, he swore silently to himself that now, at least, he had the driver trapped. Knowing the back roads of the area as he did, he knew that the lane in question was a dead end, with only one or two drives in which a driver could turn in, and no place to hide a car.

On instinct, he reached down and unclipped the restraining strap on his service revolver.

However as events turned out, Officer Scherzinger would never need to draw his weapon that night. Having momentarily lost sight of the car ahead as he made the dangerous turn, he was amazed to look ahead at the narrow lane and see only moonlight and vacant road ahead.

"You have to understand that my dad was not one for kidding around, particularly about police work," Theresa says. "He would never make up a story, but he told us kids that when he made that turn, the old Chevy ahead was just gone—vanished! He kept his flashers and siren going and turned on his brights as he drove to the end of the lane, but there was absolutely no sign of the guy. It was like he had vanished into the night."

Reaching the end of the lane, Officer Scherzinger turned around his cruiser and slowly drove back to the main road, searching for any sign of the car. He found none. By the time he arrived back at the intersection, he found another police car blocking the road, its lights flashing a dull red against the night sky. As Officer Scherzinger parked his car and slowly got out, they were joined by a third patrol officer who had heard his radio transmission and responded.

"Dad walked over to the other officers," Theresa says, "who naturally wanted to know where his perpetrator was. Dad said he had lost him, and told them the story of his chase. He told us that one of the officers, a young guy, started to kid him about being the only cop able to lose a police chase up a blind ally, but the other guy, who was a friend of my dad's, took Dad aside and calmed him down a little. I guess he was pretty rattled." Dismissing the young officer, the pair drove in tandem back down the lane to make sure that there was no sign of the vehicle.

Once more finding the roadway empty, they stopped at the far end and Robert got out to speak once more to his fellow officer and friend. Self-consciously he began to go over the sequence of events again when he was cut short by an odd comment from the second policeman.

"Dad said the guy looked at him very directly and said, 'You know, this is a weird bit of roadway. I remember when I was in training, our sergeant told me to be careful about being out here alone at night. Maybe you should talk with him.' Dad knew the sergeant in question, who was now his post commander, and said that he would talk to him. It took a couple of weeks till he could find the time, but eventually he did have the chance," Theresa recalls.

That opportunity came after roll call one evening when Robert and several other officers were in the staff room preparing for their patrols. The post commander, having just completed his briefing, came to Officer Scherzinger and asked to speak to him before commencing his patrol. Going into his office, Robert was reminded of his promise to talk about the events of the night a week or so ago, but before he could broach the subject the commander said, "So I understand you had quite a little time the other night out at Dragster Hallow."

"Darn right," came Robert's abrupt reply, "I nearly rolled my cruiser chasing after some stupid kid who got away. The weirdest thing is that I can't figure out how he got away. I had him up that old lane and…"

Before he could continue to relate his story, his commander cut him short. "Don't let it bother you too much—there are a few guys who have seen some strange stuff out there. Cars appearing and disappearing, lights in the road—we even had one rookie radio in seeing a car run smack into a tree, but the only problem was by the time we got out there, there was no crash and no car."

Before Robert could get over his bewilderment over his superior's remarks, the officer continued. "I do remember one accident that happened for real right out there," he said, a distant look in his eye.

"About twenty years or so ago, I was a rookie and got the call for backup. It was one heck of a mess. Bunch of kids joyriding went off the road and into the field just at that stretch you were describing. Flipped the car and killed everyone inside. It was enough to turn my stomach, I can tell you. The pity of it was that the kid who was driving had just bought the car that week. I guess he was out testing its limits, and he found them. I still remember it—a brand new Chevy Coup—midnight blue." Looking up from his remembrance, the commander looked very directly at Robert Scherzinger. "Let me suggest that you not talk too much about the other night. Just keep your mind on your job and don't go out to that section unless you have to." With that, his interview was over, and the story of the ghost car was etched into his memory forever.

Another striking tale told by a Hoosier policeman is related by Officer Ray Sarkkinen, a veteran of an Indianapolis area police department. Sarkkinen, a tall, imposing figure, looks very much the stereotypical figure of a rough-hewn police officer. Indeed, Ray describes himself, somewhat self-depreciatively, as "a regular mouth-breathing, knuckle-dragging cop." Yet, in speaking with him, one quickly appreciates that this description belies a man who, beneath this veneer, displays a gentle, philosophical nature.

This philosophical bent comes to the fore as he begins to speak of an event that occurred several years ago, yet remains with him to this day. As he warms to his story, it readily becomes apparent that, far from an idle incident from his past, this is a tale of great personal import for Officer Sarkkinen. It is a dramatic story that speaks of the danger that those who walk the "thin blue line" face every day, yet contained within it is a story of familial love. It is also a tale best related in his own words.

"My maternal grandfather was a brick mason by trade," he begins, "an active, intelligent man who saw life as an endless source of wonderment. He was of medium height for his generation and painfully thin. He swore he could never gain weight after being gassed in the trenches of World War I, no matter how hard Grandma tried to fatten him up.

"He was patiently locked into the deep rhythms of life...from the every-morning coffee he insisted on drinking from the saucer instead of the cup, down to the bowl of tobacco in his pipe each evening. He was an active, outdoorsy sort, who fly-fished with a rod and reel he'd bought as a teen, took his annual deer with a rifle given to him by his own father, and always had the time to tramp the woods with his grandson...but only so long as I stayed respectfully quiet in the stillness there."

Warming to his story, Ray speaks with love and warmth of the influence his grandparents, and in particular his grandfather, had on his life, an influence that he still feels today. He goes on to relate how, after returning from military service in Vietnam, he lived with his grandparents for a time while searching for his course in life. Eventually, Ray began his career in law enforcement and moved away from his grandparents' home, but not their sustaining influence.

"Fast forward to 1975 and me as an Indianapolis police patrolman," Officer Sarkkinen continues. "The pay was pretty crummy then, even lower (comparatively speaking) than cops are paid today. Like everyone else I moonlighted in order to keep ahead of my family bills. I would get up at 5 A.M., shower and drive a tri-axle dump truck until about 2 P.M. Then I would go home, quickly shower and change into my uniform and report for roll-call at the district police substation at 3 P.M. for my eight-hour shift.

"As you might well imagine, it got to be a grind every day, and I was often running at low ebb by the end of my duty shift each night. That's not the way to be when you're running a patrol beat in the busy part of town."

Indeed, one night it was that very weariness that would nearly cost Ray his life. "It was a rundown three-story apartment building," he remembers, "with a faded sign that said 'Harvey Apartments,' harkening back to a brighter time, before urban blight had overtaken that part of town. At about 10:30 P.M., the dispatcher assigned me to quiet a loud stereo on the second floor.

"The dispatcher had done me quite a favor, I recall thinking, as I could take my sweet old time in investigating the comparatively minor complaint. By the time I was finished, it would be the end of my shift, and I would be able to go home and collapse in bed for a few hours before awakening to another day on the dump truck. I had it all figured out...or thought I did.

"As I approached the apartment's door, I could readily hear the muffled thumping of the resident's bass stereo speakers, and I was going over in my mind what to say to him in my best 'Officer Friendly' manner to get him to willingly comply with the city's anti-noise ordinance. The last thing I wanted was to have to make an arrest for a noise violation as that would throw me into overtime this late in my duty shift...and all I was thinking about was sleep.

"I rapped on the door with my knuckles and got a disinterested sounding 'Come in' in response," Ray says. "As I opened the door, I saw the sole occupant of the room, a tall red-headed guy dressed in worn-out blue jeans and little else. My easy-going 'Officer Friendly' spiel seemed to fall on deaf ears as he stood there staring at me through red-rimmed, hazy blue eyes. I knew he was on speed just from looking at him and to this day swear that I could hear his molars grinding against each other as he slowly turned and picked up a 20-gauge shotgun that was leaning against a cabinet.

"I couldn't believe my eyes," Officer Sarkkinen continues, the tension of that night creeping back into his voice. "I was standing there in this doorway in full uniform, explaining that he needed to turn the music down...and he was picking up a shotgun and swinging it to bear down on me. I thought that any second now he would come to his senses and see who I was and realize that I'd be on my way with no harm done after a brief conversation. But I could see, in painfully slow motion, that he fully intended to shoot me. I even heard the audible click of him thumb-cocking the gun in preparation to fire it, even above the sound of the stereo. It somehow seemed surreal."

The tension in his voice rising, Ray continued. "Right then someone put a strong hand on my ribcage and shoved me aside toward my left so I wasn't standing there right in the middle of the apartment's doorway. I distinctly felt the thumb and first finger on my side as I was pushed to the side. Simultaneously, I heard three quick gunshots and saw the bullets impacting my red-headed attacker. A moment later I saw him crumple and fall.

"My first thought was relief...relief that another officer must have responded to my run without being assigned, had shoved me out of the line of fire and intervened with force just in the nick of time to save my hide. My next thought was to bitterly curse myself for being so stupid as to get caught standing in the 'fatal funnel' of an open doorway with a gunman inside, like a deer frozen in the headlights of an oncoming car. They had hammered us about that at the training academy, over and over, during recruit school and in-service training.

"As this humiliation washed over me, my senses were drawn toward some motion in the bottom half of my vision. I looked down, still laboring to mentally catch up with what had happened, and realized the motion I saw was my service handgun bucking upward in recoil...and realized that I was the one firing the gunshots. Still stunned and confused, but for once acting like a trained professional, I kept the suspect covered after he fell inert to the floor and then visually swept the interior of the room for other possible threats. Seeing none, I called for help with my hand-held radio and feverishly tried to slow my heart down and take stock of what had happened.

"I was alone in that second floor hallway," Ray continues. "Someone had forcibly shoved me out of the apartment's open doorway, enabling me to use the doorjamb for partial cover as I fired to defend myself. Someone shoved me out of danger and back to my senses, but yet I stood there alone, with a woman screaming in the apartment below, and the loud stereo still going and the sound of gunfire ringing in my ears. I looked up and down the hallway, still confused, with the acrid burn-smell of gunpowder in the air...and was riveted fully alert by another smell. An old and familiar one.

"It was tobacco smoke, and not just any smoke, but something I instantly recognized though I hadn't smelled it in years. The half-and-half mix of vanilla Cavendish and Burley pipe tobacco that my grandfather used. Thoughts of him washed over me as I stood there, so strongly that I remembered the last time I'd spoken to him before his death several years before. Just as quickly as I noticed the smell of his pipe tobacco, it was gone, driven from my senses by the sound of sirens pounding in the distance and the realities of what had happened."

As Ray draws his story toward its conclusion, the tension begins to ease from his voice and his eyes regain their customary gentle twinkle. "You'll probably guess that I wondered if my grandfather had somehow managed to shove me to safety and back to my senses, despite his being deceased for perhaps four years when that shooting incident occurred. You'd be right, too...I did just that for quite some time. I even told my wife and a couple of close friends about it.

"But cops don't feel at ease with thoughts like that. Especially when we're trained that when suddenly confronted with danger the human animal, like any other animal, will do one of three things...fight, flee, or freeze. That's what it was, surely...I just froze up because I didn't have my mind on the job as I should have.

"Still, that logic fails to explain how I managed to get un-froze and save myself, instead of simply dying right there in my shoes as violent crime victims sometimes do, even when they have the means to defend themselves. It also fails to account for the sensation I felt of a hand shoving me to safety. Or for the smell of that particular blend of pipe tobacco that night."

Officer Sarkkinen goes on to relate that, despite his wounds, the offender did indeed recover to face legal charges of assault on an officer. Ray returned to duty, wiser for his close call. However, the experience of that evening has left an indelible impression on him.

On first hearing, one might be tempted to simply dismiss Officer Sarkkinen's story as, at least, a bizarre incident that may be written off as a psychological reaction to a stressful situation. However, Ray offers a postscript to his story that might suggest such experiences are not as impossibly uncommon as they might seem.

"Many years have passed, of course," he now relates, a wry smile crossing his face, "but I recently spent some time with a buddy who retired from the New York City Police Department. We reminisced about things that have happened to us during our long careers, and I eventually shared with him the story I've just recounted to you. To my astonishment, he shook his head in a knowing assent and told me that something similar had happened to him during an armed robbery stake-out in a jewelry store.

"He told me that he and two other cops were waiting to apprehend an especially violent stick-up artist. When the bad guy appeared, my friend, a young officer at the time, stepped out from behind a display case and confronted the armed robber at gunpoint. He thought he had to do so because his supervisor told him to give the criminal a chance to surrender."

Ray continues, "The hold-up man's response was to whirl toward the young officer and fire. My friend told me, 'Just as he started to turn toward me, I felt someone behind me grab my shoulders with both hands and jerk me back behind the cover of the display case. I was so grateful as it kept me from getting killed...but when I turned to see who had saved me, I saw no one was there.' My friend told me that a feeling came over him that it was his father who had pulled him to safety. The trouble is, he had buried his father the previous week."

So the stories go, from officer to officer, department to department. Each story is as individual as the officer who tells it, yet together they weave an eerie tapestry of tales, coming from a profession that some would consider an odd source of supernatural tales.

Yet perhaps it is not so surprising that those who proudly wear a badge would be the bearers of such stories. By the very nature of their work, dealing with the drama of life and death every day, perhaps they are brought closer to the mystery of whatever lies behind the veiled curtain of life and death. Perhaps it is the utter reality of their chosen profession that also makes them prone to experience what some might consider the more enigmatic side of our life. Whatever the case, from within the ranks of the "thin blue line," strange stories are told. They are an often-overlooked part of the lore of professional police work, and an indispensable part of Hoosier ghostlore.

8
THE GHOSTLY GUESTS OF FRANKLIN

Franklin, Indiana looks and feels like the quintessential small Midwestern city. Strolling through this picturesque community, one is quickly impressed with a sense of hometown charm and warmth. Franklin, like so many of the towns and cities dotting the Indiana landscape, seems to exude a wholesome atmosphere that is atypical in the onrush of modern American life. In such an idyllic setting, it is hard to imagine that one is just twenty miles from the center of downtown Indianapolis.

Franklin, a city of twenty thousand residents, seems very much the model of what a small city can be. Large enough to allow for modern conveniences, it is still the sort of place where families sit on front porches on summer evenings and mothers push strollers down tree-lined downtown streets.

The city can trace its roots to 1823, seven short years after Indiana was admitted as the nineteenth state in the Union. In that year, five newly appointed county commissioners met in the home of John Smiley, a settler who lived in a small community along Sugar Creek. The previous year, the Indiana State Legislature had carved out the boundaries of Johnson County and the purpose of this meeting was to determine the site for the county seat.

The seeds planted at this meeting came to fruition in the coming years as the Village of Franklin, as it was soon named, grew into a prosperous center of commerce and settlement. Ten years after its founding, the *Indiana Gazetteer* described the town as:

> ...a post town and the seat of justice of Johnson County, situated on the state road leading from Columbus to Indianapolis and near the center of the county. It stands on a high bluff on the east bank of Young's Creek surrounded by a body of as rich land as any in the state and contains a population of two hundred and fifty souls, four mercantile stores, two taverns, two physicians and a number of mechanics of various kinds.

Though time has wrought its changes to the community, somehow the town has maintained some of the sturdy character implanted in it by its settler forbearers. In towns and cities like Franklin, values and traditions are still very much a part of life.

Perhaps this explains the fact that this is a city seemingly replete with ghostly tales. Far from the dark denizens commonly depicted in horror movies, these specters are as much a part of hometown life as high school football games and community Thanksgiving food drives. Their presence in Franklin has been noted for generations until they have become a part of the very fabric of the city.

If one were to take a ghostly tour of this most haunted of Indiana cities, a good place to begin would be the lovely Victorian home of Kathy Harlow, a single mother of two. Located on a quiet street not far from downtown, this charming house sits gracefully serene. Within its walls, however, it seems that things may, at moments, be surprisingly lively. This might be expected from a home that houses two energetic young boys, but according to the stories told of the place, it seems that not all the activity in this home can be attributed to the living members of the family residing there. In this elegant dwelling, a part of the life comes from a distinctly "dead" source.

Exact records on the home are not readily available, but some sense of its history is known. It is believed that it was built in the early 1880s, designed by a local architect named Butler. Constructed as a classic example of Victorian architecture, the two-story home boasts a wraparound porch on the outside and a spacious, comfortable interior. The house originally contained four family bedrooms plus living quarters for a butler upstairs with formal drawing and dining rooms as well as a full kitchen downstairs. With cherry-stained woodwork throughout the house, this charming home was built to reflect the refined tastes of those who would inhabit it. For the first twenty years of its existence, the house served as a private residence until it was purchased for use as a YMCA for Franklin College in the early 1900s.

Sometime in the mid-twentieth century, the home was reconverted for use as a residence. It seems to have passed through the hands of a number of owners until a local physician purchased it in the 1970s. Finally, the house was left vacant, silent and empty for at least two years prior to Kathy purchasing the home in 2002.

Ms. Harlow, who has a keen interest in history and folklore, seems to feel a natural affinity for her home that becomes clear whenever she speaks of it. As she tells the tale of how she came to purchase the venerable old mansion, she muses that she was somehow fated to own it.

"I moved to Franklin in 1988," she now remembers, "and every day I would pass by this house on my way to work. I loved the wraparound porch and the general look of the place. I have always dreamed of owning a 'Victorian Lady,' but of course I assumed that it would always be just that—a dream. Even when I saw that the house was empty and for sale, I thought that it would be way beyond my means to buy it.

"Then," she continues, "one night I had a dream that I had purchased this house for a ridiculously low amount of money. I woke up and thought, 'That was totally cool,' but I knew that there was no way that it could happen."

Something of the dream must have remained with Kathy, however, for she reports that several weeks later she was suddenly overcome with an impulse to inquire about the house. "I called and the realtor told me the price and I thought, 'OK, this is way beyond my means,' but I agreed to go over and see the place just for the fun of it," she explains.

What followed was a rather unusual real estate transaction when the current owner of the beautiful old Victorian offered to purchase her current house, thereby making her purchase more affordable. "When it was all said and done, I purchased and moved into this house in about two weeks—for exactly the amount I had dreamed I would pay for it," Kathy recalls with a smile.

It was at the house closing that Ms. Harlow received her first notion that there might be more to the house than just a stately old home. "I was sitting at the closing table and all the papers were signed," she remembers. Since Kathy has also harbored a lifelong interest in ghosts and ghostlore, she decided to broach what turned out to be a fateful question. "Just for the fun of it, I turned to the former owners and asked, 'Oh, by the way, are there any ghost stories attached to this house?'

"Suddenly everyone at the table froze and their eyes got big. Somebody finally sort of stammered, 'No, of course NOT!' Needless to say, with that reaction, I knew that there was something they weren't saying, so I responded, 'No, it's OK, I actually enjoy ghost stories, so it's OK to tell me.' The former owner's wife looked at me for a long minute and then kind of blurted out, 'OK, yes, we have had some experiences in this house—but it's a good ghost! We think it's a little boy.'"

Fascinated, Kathy listened as the woman told her of some of their experiences in the home. "She said it was good ghost because sometimes he would do little favors for them," Kathy recalls. "She said that at times when she would leave her bed undone, she would come home to find it had been made. She also said there were several times when they would come home late at night, and as they walked up to the door, all the lights would go on in the house like he was welcoming them home."

The former owner also told a story of coming home late one night to find that she had inadvertently locked her house keys inside when she had left some hours earlier. According to her story, as she stood on the porch, unsure of how she would gain entrance to the locked home, she heard the sound of the door being unlocked from inside. A moment later she tried the door again to find it unlocked.

As eerie as these tales might be, the woman was saving her best story for last. "She said that when she first moved into the house, her son was three or four years old," Kathy relates. Like many young boys of that age, this child soon developed an imaginary friend that he would play with for hours on end. His mother, understanding that this was a natural stage for a child to go through, thought nothing of it until one day when an incident occurred that caused her to question her assumption.

"The front bedroom was this little boy's room," Ms. Harlow continues, "and she would be downstairs and could hear him upstairs giggling and playing and talking about the friend he was playing with. Then one day, when she was upstairs in the master bedroom, she could hear the little boy talking away. She suddenly realized that it sounded like a conversation—not just jabbering, but a back-and-forth cadence to what he was saying. She didn't hear anything being said in response to her son's comments, but he would pause like there was a conversation going on."

Now suddenly feeling a tinge of uneasiness, the mother left her room to go down the hall and look in on the youngster. What she saw was more than a little startling. Peeking in the door at her son, she saw him sitting on the floor, his legs spread in a "V" with a small rubber ball on the floor before him. As he continued to happily talk to his unseen friend, he reached out and rolled the ball forward toward the empty room. Transfixed, the woman watched while the ball rolled several feet along the floor, suddenly stopped and then rolled back toward her son. "That's when it got her attention," Ms. Harlow remarks. "That's when she decided that she had a ghost in the house."

The former owner concluded her story that day by adding that she had done some historical research on the house and found that a former owner of the home had suffered the death of a child while living there. As it would later prove significant, he was killed while riding a bicycle in the street in front of the home.

While such news regarding a home they had just purchased might give most people reason to question their acquisition, it seems that this revelation did not faze Ms. Harlow. "I have always loved ghost stories and have done some ghost research myself, so it didn't bother me," she now admits. "In fact, I really didn't think about it too much."

She decided not to mention anything about what she had been told to her two young sons, aged fourteen and twelve, and soon her thoughts were swept up in a flurry of activity. The days immediately after purchasing the Victorian house were spent busily packing in happy preparation for her move. About two weeks later, however, with the actual process of moving her family's belongings underway, she would be given reason to remember those words again.

"Shortly after starting to move in, I was alone in the house one afternoon," she remembers with a smile. "I was standing in the parlor surrounded by all of these packing boxes when I began to realize that I was feeling uncomfortable. It was this generalized feeling that somehow I was not alone in the house—that something or someone was watching me. So, I went through the house and simply started talking. I said, out loud, 'My name is Kathy and I'm moving in now. I'm Mom.' Then I went back to the living room and started to hang curtains."

In spite of, or perhaps because of her comments to the unseen presence in the house, Ms. Harlow soon seemed to receive confirmation that she was not alone. "After hanging curtains for a few minutes, I suddenly heard a metallic sound coming from the basement. I instinctively knew what it was—the sound of a metal bucket I had left down there being scooted across the cement floor. I knew for a fact that I was alone in the house so I decided to leave right then and there."

Kathy reports that as she and her sons continued the process of moving their belongings into their new home, her sense of comfort in the home increased. At odd moments, however, she still had hints that there was another—unseen—presence in their midst.

"One of the first things I did as we moved in was to hang curtains all over the house," she now recalls. "The problem was that every morning I would come downstairs to find all the kitchen curtains on the floor. Since the curtains were on rods and the rods were still hung, intact, they could not simply slip off. It was as though they had intentionally been removed."

Routinely, Ms. Harlow would replace the curtains each morning only to find them on the floor again the next day. "I even started getting creative, trying to find a way to keep them up," she explains. "At one point I got packing tape and taped them to the window, but sure enough, the next morning they had been torn down and were lying on the floor."

In vain, Kathy looked for some explanation for the errant behavior of the kitchen curtains. "It occurred to me that it could be our cats but if they were responsible, their claws would have left marks in the curtains and the curtains themselves looked untouched. Besides, how could the cats take down the curtains without taking down the rods?"

Finally, unsure of just what she could do to address the problem, she chose to address what she perceived to be the source of the happenings. "One morning after about two weeks, I came down to find, once again, that the curtains had been taken down during the night," she describes. "Finally, I had enough. Out loud I said to whatever was doing this, 'Stop it! Enough is enough. Look, your joke is funny and I appreciate it and everything, but things are different now. We have to have curtains stay up. I'm Mom and I'm telling you right now to stop it!' It must have had some effect because from that moment on the curtains stayed up."

Despite the odd goings on, Kathy Harlow still chose to avoid telling her two sons about the possibility that their new home could be haunted. "I didn't want my sons to be scared about their new house," she remarks. Still, as she was about to learn, even her good intentions could not insulate her children from the odd occurrences in the home.

According to Kathy, one morning a couple of weeks after her family had moved in, she was in the kitchen making dinner when her youngest son Nicholas came down the back stairs and announced, "Mom, I think this house is haunted!" As causally as she could, Kathy asked, "Really, what makes you say that?"

"Because I see things," he simply stated. When Kathy pressed him for more details, he explained, "I see a bicycle, going along the wall of my bedroom. I see it out of the corner of my eye and then it's gone." Pausing for a moment, the boy then added one detail that Kathy found both fascinating and chilling. "But one thing about the bicycle—it is all crushed up and wrecked!"

"Now that got my attention," Kathy Harlow remembers, "because of what the former owner had told me about the child who had lived here being killed in a bicycle accident. At that point I knew that it was time to talk to my boys."

As gently as she could, Kathy told her sons what she had learned about the history of the house as well as the incidents that had happened to her. To her relief, the boys took the news in stride, not seeming to be particularly concerned about the spectral presence in their home.

Since that time, Kathy and her sons have come to accept their "resident ghost" as part and parcel of their charming home. "Most of the time, the incidents are little, almost playful," Kathy reports. "Once, within the first year of moving in, my boys and I were pulling out of the driveway to leave for the day when I happened to glance back at the house and saw that the front curtain was pulled up, as though someone was behind the window watching us leave. I pointed it out to the boys and we all waved goodbye as we drove away. When we got back that night, the curtain was back in its place."

At other times, whatever spirit seems to linger in the home has been a bit more obvious in indicating its presence. "About six months ago," Kathy remembers, "in the fall of 2004, my son Michael and a friend told me that they were walking through the kitchen when they saw a ball of light bouncing around the room. On other occasions, both of my boys have heard their names called when no one was around, and recently, I heard a child's voice call out to me saying, 'Hi!' as though someone wanted to get my attention. It happens infrequently but still enough that we have gotten used to it."

At least once, the spectral child has been seen rather than merely heard or felt in the home. "At one point a few years ago, my boys had a friend staying with us for a few days," Kathy describes. "One night, the three of them were playing hide-and-seek in the house and my son and his friend came downstairs to the laundry room looking for my other son. They swore to me that when they walked into the room, they saw a boy they didn't recognize standing there looking at them smiling. Then suddenly, he was just gone—vanished!"

It seems that in this genteel, elegant home, located on a quiet street not far from downtown Franklin, something mysterious continues to make its presence known in both subtle and obvious ways. Maybe, as Kathy Harlow believes, it is the unquiet spirit of a child who was taken from this life before his time. If this is the case, then perhaps he has finally found his place in this loving family. One might hope that this has brought him a measure of peace that was denied him in a life cut short.

If the spirit of a young boy truly walks the halls of this beautiful old home, then it can be said that he is not the only ghostly resident of Franklin. As one begins to delve into the lore of this fascinating city, one finds a legion of specters that call this quaint city home.

Stories that have been told for many years suggest that at least two ghosts are attached to the halls of Franklin College. If the tales are true, then these spirits may be considered fortunate, for one could not wish for a more refined, congenial spot to while away an afterlife than within the ivy covered walls of this institution.

This four-year liberal arts college was founded in 1834 by members of the Baptist church in Indiana. Initially founded as the Indiana Baptist Manual Labor Institute, the seventy-four-acre campus, lined with tall trees and shaded walkways, looks very much the part of a beautiful, traditional midwestern college. The air of the campus bustles with the sound of young laughter and the flurry of students rushing to class. Lingering in the shadows of this wholesome atmosphere, however, there lies a more macabre aspect to college life. For, sifting through the myriad of tales told at and about this college, one finds a pair of ghosts said to haunt these hallowed halls.

One of the oldest and most well-known of the Franklin College ghosts is said to be that of a hapless coed who died a violent and untimely death at the college many years ago. The details of how this young woman met her death seem to vary with each retelling of the tale; however, most of the stories originate in the early part of the last century in a former dormitory called Bryan Hall. Bryan Hall, which was built in 1908, served the campus as a dormitory for seventy-seven years until its fiery destruction in 1985.

In the early 1920s, Bryan Hall was home to many sororities. It is said that the ill-fated young woman, a freshman at the time, was a member of one of these organizations who had a falling out with her upper-classman roommate and fellow sorority sister. According to some variants of the story, the cause of their quarrel was a boy who had been courting both women. While this situation alone was enough to raise tensions between the two roommates, that spring, when one lost and one won the heart of their young swain, their clash came to a violent culmination. It is said that in a fit of homicidal anger, the older girl produced a knife, murdered the younger girl and then proceeded to dismember the body and place it behind a loose piece of paneling in the wall of the room.

When the young girl failed to show up at classes the next week, her former roommate told friends that she had suddenly decided to quit school and had returned home. By the time the semester ended some weeks later, her sudden disappearance had been largely forgotten.

According to the legend, it was not until that summer when a custodian, cleaning Bryan Hall in the absence of students, noted an odd smell emanating from a room on the second floor. Concerned, he called maintenance workers who removed the paneling from the walls and made a grisly discovery.

The legends are vague regarding the fate of the culprit. Some suggest that she was never found while others say she was confined to a mental institution. However, what most of the stories are specific about is that pains were taken to cover up the death of the girl. According to campus lore, school officials had her picture removed from the campus yearbooks and all references to her death deleted from school records.

However, according to the legends that floated through the campus for many years thereafter, the spirit of the murdered girl refused to be erased so easily from the school. For, throughout the ensuing generations of students passing through the doors of Bryan Hall, strange stories have been told. Stories of an unquiet spirit said to inhabit the second floor of the dormitory.

Jim Howard, who came to Franklin College as a freshman in 1975, lived in Bryan Hall his first year there. "Within the first two weeks of moving into the second floor, we (my roommates and I) started hearing from upperclassmen about the fact that we lived on the haunted floor," he now recalls with a smile. "When we asked about the story, we were told that two members of a sorority got into a fight there in the 1920s or 1930s and one cut the other up with a knife and put her in a wall of the room. According to the story, ever since then, people would hear this girl knocking or crying and sometimes people would see her in the hall.

"Of course," he continues, "we all thought the story was a hoot. We laughed it off and, at worst, would try to pull pranks on one another and blame it on the ghost. None of us really thought that it was possible that there was a ghost hanging around. Our room was such a mess that it would have scared any ghost, particularly a girl ghost, off in a hurry."

Before the end of the year, Jim would have at least one occasion to wonder if he and his friends were too hasty in their rejection of the ghostly stories. "That year, I didn't get to go home for spring break and got permission to stay in the dorm for the week so that I could keep my off-campus job," Jim remembers. "It was a little unnerving because I was the only one in that section of the dorm but it didn't bother me too much—at first.

"Then, on Saturday night I went out for a couple of beers with one of the other guys who was still on campus. We had one or two drinks, and I was back in the dorm by half past ten. I studied for about an hour and then went to bed, but as I tried to sleep, I became conscious of a knocking sound coming from down the hall. It was not the standard bangs that the old furnace system had; it was more of a rhythmic pounding.

"I thought at first that someone was pounding on the outside door downstairs trying to get in, but after a few minutes I realized that the knocking was coming from someplace a lot closer. I got up and followed the sound down the hall and realized that it was coming from a room at the end of the hall. It sounded like someone beating against the wall. I couldn't figure out what could be making the noise—I knew the guys who stayed in that room were gone."

Wondering if he should call the maintenance department or perhaps even campus security, Jim stood in the hall for a few moments until the mysterious sounds ceased as suddenly as they had begun. Jim continued to stand outside the door for another few moments and then, hearing nothing more from the other side, turned to go back to his room. As he did so, however, he heard one more sound from within the room.

"It was a soft crying, like a girl was inside quietly sobbing her heart out," he describes. "Now I was really spooked, but I screwed up all my courage and knocked on the door as hard as I could, but I got no response." The crying continued for another few seconds and then faded away, leaving only the silence of an empty dormitory.

As Jim now looks back at the situation, he reflects, "I probably should have called security just to make sure the room was really empty, but all I could think of was the story about the ghost of the girl who had been murdered on that floor, and suddenly, there was no way I could stay there that night. I absolutely ran back to my room, grabbed a few things, called the buddy I had been out with earlier that evening and told him that I was coming over to sleep on his floor. I never even told my roommates what happened because I knew they would just laugh at me."

Whatever the reaction of his friends might have been, many students staying in Bryan Hall and, indeed, the entire campus community, came to hear of the ghostly murder victim. A few even claimed encounters with her. Often the stories centered around hearing a knocking or scratching coming from within the walls, while other tales told of a shadowy woman seen in the hallway outside one room on the second floor who seemed to melt away into the darkness when approached. So famous did the story become that it eventually spread from the campus into the surrounding community. The story appeared in numerous local newspaper articles and was even featured in an edition of the *Indiana Folklore Journal* in the mid-1970s.

It should be clearly noted that no records exist to support the belief that a murder ever occurred on campus. Moreover, at least one faculty member, who has studied the story in depth, suggests a more prosaic explanation for the origin of the legend. According to him, the rumor of the murdered student began in the 1930s, when a female student became pregnant out of wedlock. Rather than face the shame of public scrutiny, the girl's family whisked her from the campus without notice or fanfare. In the face of her sudden disappearance, a rumor began to circulate that she had been the victim of foul play. From that point, the tale took on a life of its own. Whatever the truth of the tale and however questionable its origins, what can be stated clearly is that by the time Bryan Hall was destroyed by fire in 1985, the legend of its ghostly resident was firmly imbedded in campus lore.

As famous as this story has become, the specter of the hapless coed is not the only other worldly tale associated with the college. Another well-known ghost bears the genial name Charlie and has been spoken of around the campus for many years. His haunting ground is the campus theater, located in the Old Main building. The theater itself, which has been used for many years for lectures, music recitals and countless plays, has long been known to students as "The Gut."

While the origins of Charlie's presence have been lost in the mists of time, at least one legend suggests he is the spirit of a French student (or perhaps professor) who is said to have hung himself in the campus bell tower in the late 1800s. No campus records exist to substantiate such an event, much less provide an exact date or name of the unfortunate suicide victim. While the basis of this apparition may be murky at best, his activities within the Gut have been recorded for some time.

According to a campus newspaper article in 1975, a few years previously an unnamed male student had an unnerving encounter with Charlie late one evening within the dark recesses of the theater. The young man, a promising music student, reportedly went to the theater late one night to practice piano for an upcoming recital. As he sat at the grand piano on stage, abjectly concentrating on the Chopin piece before him, suddenly his focus was interrupted in an frightening manner. Out of the darkness of the stage, a strange face suddenly loomed over the piano, sneering in apparent disapproval of his musical expertise. Startled out of his reverie, the young man abandoned his practice and quickly retreated from the stage.

A few years later, another student came to the empty theater one night on a similar pursuit. According to the tale reported in the campus newspaper, *The Franklin*, this student used the same piano to soothe the stress of his day by pounding out some rhythm and blues tunes. As he began to lose himself in the works of Ray Charles and Dave Brubeck, he gradually became aware of an impression of presence with him on the stage. With a rising sense of unease, he realized that the hair on the back of his hands, as they pounded on the ivory keys, was standing up. In vain the young man tried to reassure himself that he was alone, though the feeling of someone close by was becoming increasingly overpowering.

Suddenly, a deep, resonant voice in his ear, rising above the sound of the piano, commanded, "Get out!" Turning toward the sound, the student was confronted with nothing but empty darkness. Like his fellow music aficionado years before, this student also chose the better part of valor and hurriedly left the theater for the safety of his dormitory.

Through the years, other students have also reported encounters with the enigmatic phantom. One coed drama student, sitting before a mirror in the dressing room while preparing for a performance, related the distinct feeling of a hand being placed on her shoulder. Thinking a fellow actress had entered the room, she turned in that direction only to find the room apparently vacant.

It seems that throughout Franklin College, like the city it occupies, ghostly tales abound. One day several years ago, a local townsperson was strolling by Province Park, adjacent to the college, when she noticed young people sitting on the grass apparently enjoying the summer day with a picnic. Upon drawing closer to the group, however, she was surprised and amazed to find that they were all wearing garments of the late nineteenth or early twentieth century. Needless to say, no sort of historical reenactment was going on that day and no explanation for why a costumed group of students would be picnicking could be found. In the end, the local woman was left with the impression that she had somehow seen a ghostly vision of an event from nearly one hundred years ago.

In any other town, such a public display of ghostly bravado might be considered a bit conspicuous. However, as one reviews the rolls of the uncannily lively sprits of Franklin, it seems that the ethereal picnickers might feel quite at home.

Several other prominent buildings in Franklin boast their own resident specters. The Artcraft Theater, on Franklin's Main Street, has been the center of strange rumors for many years. This venerable theater, built in 1922, has been a hub of community life in Franklin for decades. Generations of Franklin residents whiled away their hours in the cloistered darkness within its walls. As a *Johnson County Daily Journal* article noted in 2004, "The 81-year-old theater…has been a constant in the lives of many local residents, as they grew from wide-eyed youngsters to lovey-dovey teens to parents with children of their own." Indeed, the Artcraft even enjoyed a moment of national attention when it was prominently featured in a 1940 *Life* magazine photo spread on Franklin entitled, "A Small Town's Saturday Night."

Attending events at the Artcraft, which served for so long as part of the heartbeat of this city, is truly a tradition in Franklin. Perhaps it is only apropos that part of that tradition has been sharing strange tales of mysterious happenings throughout the theater.

Many of the tales centered around the concession stand, where tubs of popcorn have been known to fly off the counter as though shoved by an invisible hand and a soda machine repeatedly turns itself on and off without human aid. Interestingly, these phenomena are said to have begun shortly after the death of an employee known as "the popcorn lady," who had served her community from the refreshment stand at the Artcraft for more than thirty-seven years.

However, the phantom or phantoms of the Artcraft do not confine their eerie activity to the refreshment stand. Strange whisperings have been reported from the auditorium when no customers were present and odd music is said to have been heard emanating from the projection booth. Even more directly, an employee reported seeing a pair of disembodied legs casually strolling down a hall before disappearing into the wall at the opposite end. While cleaning up after a show, another employee reported seeing a ghostly hand waving to him from the darkness of the auditorium. Perhaps it was a friendly spirit simply sending a greeting.

Next to the Artcraft Theater, the Willard Restaurant offers great food, a warm atmosphere and quite possibly more than its fair share of "spirits." Both customers and staff at the fine dining establishment have long whispered tales of an attractive female spirit who seems to enjoy frequenting the establishment. According to a *Daily Journal* article, this specter is often seen in the hallway just outside the bar, dressed in a long white gown. Prominent witnesses have seen her glance toward the bar area and then proceed down the hall, yet before she reaches the end, she simply vanishes. Startled customers have been known to run to the area where she had just been seen, looking for an explanation of her disappearance only to be disappointed...and more than a little uneasy when none could be found.

According to the stories, this elusive feminine spirit does not always remain in the hallway. At least one bartender has seen her in the bar area. According to his tale, he was preparing the bar for business early one weekend morning when he looked up from his work to find himself face to face with a young woman in a long dress. Shocked, because the Willard would not be open for another hour, the young bartender was about to ask the woman how she had gotten in when she smiled, turned and silently glided from the bar into the hall. When he followed a moment later, he found the area empty. He then confirmed that all the outside doors were locked and searched the entire building without finding any sign of his attractive and puzzling visitor.

Bob Schofield, who purchased the Willard in 1999, was quoted in the *Daily Journal* admitting that while he has never personally seen the ghost, he has, on at least one occasion, distinctly felt her presence. As he told the *Journal*, "We definitely have some...things going on around this place. I really think there is something. I don't disbelieve in things like that."

Who this enigmatic presence might be remains a mystery. One old tale suggests that many years ago, long before the building was remodeled into a restaurant, it was the home of two women, both of whom were heavily involved in the temperance movement and proponents of prohibition. It has been suggested that the ghost currently said to inhabit the Willard is that of one of these women coming to show her disapproval with the sale of alcohol in her former home. However, at least one regular at the Willard takes a different view on this story. "Maybe the reason she is standing out there in the hall," he surmises, "is because she is looking in at all the fun she missed out on in life!"

Perhaps the most colorful ghost of Franklin is attached to one of the more intriguing buildings in town. Known as the "Masonic Temple Building," today it is the home of the Johnson County Museum of History. Appropriately, this organization, dedicated to the preservation of local history, is housed in this expansive site, a building itself rich in history and lore.

The roots of this singular building can be traced to January 1850, when local resident Fabius Finch and eight other men organized a group that would shortly become chartered as "Franklin Masonic Lodge #107 of the Free and Accepted Masons." Free Masonry was a growing fraternal organization in Indiana at the time and the lodge grew quickly, having to move their meeting locations several times in the process. By the early 1900s, the group had grown large enough that it was obvious to all that a more spacious and permanent location would have to be secured. In 1919, the group purchased a lot in the downtown section of Franklin and three years later ground was broken for the Masonic Temple.

By the time the ornate new building was dedicated on April 14, 1924, the project bore impressive fruit. Designed by Evansville architect Clifford Shopbell, the 30,000 square foot building is a striking example of Neo-classical style with Ionic columns gracing the exterior and strong, graceful lines throughout the interior. Built for $104,000, which was considered a fortune at the time, the building is tastefully ornate from the meeting rooms to the large auditorium used for Masonic rites and presentations.

Throughout the ensuing years, the Masonic Temple continued the use for which it was originally designed but also evolved into a community center for the city of Franklin as well. The funeral of Franklin resident Martin Short, who had served as Consul General of the United States to Turkey, was held in the auditorium since it was the only space large enough in the area to house the number of mourners attending. During World War II, the temple became the headquarters for the local chapter of the American Red Cross who used it for blood drives as well as for packing surgical dressings and soldiers' kit bags destined for the battlefronts. The building has also been the site of countless banquets, meetings of service organizations and even high school proms.

Throughout the years, however, the cost of maintaining the mammoth facility became unfeasible, and in July 1988, the building was purchased in a cooperative venture by Johnson County and the Johnson County Historical Society for use as an historical museum. Realizing the significance of the building they had purchased, the historical society took great care in their renovation not to change the structure of the building itself while updating and improving the heating, electrical and lighting throughout the grand old structure. In 1991, shortly after the Masonic Temple was officially placed on the National Registry of Historic Places, the Johnson County Museum of History moved into its new home. Since that time, further improvements have been made, including a 1.5 million dollar renovation in 2002. Still, the mystique, charm and ambiance of the building remain much as they have been since its construction some eighty years ago.

To journey through the museum today is to take a fascinating step back into Johnson County and Indiana history. Artifacts and exhibits display the social, political and historical roots of the area. The extensive genealogy department is a favorite site for those seeking their personal ancestry and the museum is a frequent destination of school groups searching for a way to make history come alive for the students. It is both appropriate and significant that the venue for this impressive collection of memorabilia is a vast historical monument itself. The very atmosphere of the building seems imbued with an aura of wonder and mystery; the walls quietly reverberate the memory of ceremonies and rituals unfamiliar to the general public. It is only natural that such a location is the favorite haunt of one of the more intriguing local ghosts.

She is known simply as the "Lady in White," and her presence was first noted in the auditorium section of the building. Ben Jason,* a resident of the nearby Masonic Home, was an active member of Masonic Lodge #107 for many years and remembers hearing stories of the Lady in White when he first became a member.

"I became active in the Masons in the late 1950s," Ben now explains, warming to his recollections. "I was a few years out of the service and working at a store downtown, and a couple of my friends had joined, so they kind of dragged me along. It was a great organization to be a part of and we did a great deal of good for the community over the years.

"When I was first inducted," he continues, "I was given a grand tour of the place. When we got to the auditorium where we held most of our rites, the old guy showing me around said, 'Now you have to be a little careful in this place when it's dark or when no one else is around. There is a spook who lives in here and she doesn't like to be disturbed.' Of course, I thought he was kidding me, but the more I heard people talk, the more I began to wonder.

"The first time I started to think there was more than just a story to all this came a few months later after one of our meetings when a couple of the guys and I were having coffee. We started talking about the temple and one of my buddies cracked a joke about the ghost. Another older fella at the table looked at him very sternly and said, 'Don't joke about our Lady in White—she's real and a lot of us have seen her.' There was something about his look that made us shut up and listen."

As Mr. Jason and his friends sat entranced, the older member told of coming into the auditorium one evening several years earlier to set up for a presentation that would take place that night. As he unlocked the door to the room, he was shocked to glance at the stage and see, standing to one side next to the curtain, the diaphanous form of a woman in a long white dress. Wondering how someone could have entered the locked building before he arrived, he was about to ask the woman who she was when he noticed an astonishing aspect to the figure.

"He told us that she had no legs or feet," Ben Jason now recalls. "He was adamant that below her gown there were no legs—she just sort of faded away. Then he said as he stood there staring at her bug-eyed, she sort of floated to the center of the stage and just faded away. In a second she was just gone." Ben remarks that in a different setting, he and his friends might have been tempted to laugh off the story as a joke or hallucination of some sort, but the obvious sincerity of their lodge brother quickly silenced these inclinations.

This wouldn't be the only time that Ben Jason would hear of encounters with the Lady in White. On another occasion in the mid-1960s, it was one of Ben's close friends who reported a strange incident in the auditorium. "One night, before a performance we had that summer," Ben remembers, "a friend and I were backstage talking when suddenly my friend asked, 'Do you ever feel uneasy in this place when you are alone?' I thought it was a strange question and told him that I never really thought about it, but he said 'Well, I sure as heck do and I don't think I am going to come here alone anymore if I can avoid it!'"

Intrigued, Ben asked what would make him arrive at this decision, and in response his friend told him an eerie tale. He related that late the night before, he had come to the lodge by himself to practice a long recitation that he had to memorize for that night's presentation. As he stood alone on the stage, concentrating on his monologue, suddenly the silence of the auditorium was broken by the sound of footsteps proceeding up the main aisle toward the stage. Thinking it strange that anyone else would be in the building at that late hour and that he had not heard the outer door to the auditorium open, the man stopped his practice and called out, asking who was there.

No answer was given to his question, but the light footsteps continued to proceed toward him. A thrill of apprehension creeping through him, the man waited in silence till the footsteps approached the stage, yet no shape became visible through the darkness. Then, silence reigned again in the auditorium. After a few moments, he managed to regain control of his fear and tried to convince himself that he had merely been hearing the usual creeks and groans of an old building. After a moment, he forced himself to resume his practice. Shortly, however, his recitation was again interrupted by the sound of footsteps. Once again, they began at the far end of the main aisle and retraced their path toward the stage.

By now completely unnerved, the lodge member yelled into the ambient air, demanding to know who was in the auditorium. Once again, his query was met only with silence. Unsure of what to do, the man stood in stunned immobility as the sound of the phantom foot treads approached the stage and then stopped. Deciding that it was time to leave the area without delay, he turned to make his way to the side entrance when a stage light overhead suddenly clicked on, its harsh brilliance cutting through the darkness. In its illumination he could clearly see he was alone in the auditorium. Now deciding to make his retreat by the closest possible route, the gentleman unceremoniously leapt from the stage, landed in the aisle and ran from the building.

Ben Jason now says that as he listened to his friend's tale, he recalled the old story of the Lady in White that he had heard many years before. However, he was still unsure of just what to believe about the presence of a ghost in their temple. Within a month of hearing this story, he was to make up his mind.

"It was late that next fall," he now recalls. "We had had a meeting, and the guy who usually locked the building up was out of town, so a couple of us were going through the building, shutting off lights and making sure all the doors were secure. When we got to the auditorium door, I saw that all the lights were out; I was about to close the door and lock it when I saw something out of the corner of my eye. I turned and saw something white on the main floor in front of the stage. I looked and there was a kind of shimmering white mist floating along the floor. It didn't really have a form as such and at first, I was afraid it was smoke but I could see from the way it hung together and kind of glowed that it wasn't any kind of smoke I had ever seen. Then, it started moving."

As Ben now remembers, the mist seemed to collect itself and began moving slowly and purposely up the main aisle toward him. "I was too shocked to move at first," he admits, "but when it got about halfway down the aisle, my fear took over and I yelled and ran out, slamming the door as I went." Ben now says that as he quickly left the auditorium, he nearly toppled over another lodge member who was helping close the building and had heard his shout a moment before. Stammering out an explanation and description of what he had seen, Ben felt his sense of panic beginning to ebb. After a moment, his friend convinced Ben to go back with him to the auditorium to make sure that there was no smoke or fire. With some trepidation, Ben opened the door to the auditorium once again and entered to find it empty and dark. Together the pair searched the entire area but no explanation could be found for what Ben had witnessed. "From that moment on," Ben states flatly, "I was a believer in our ghost. No more evidence was needed."

Ben Jason is not alone in his feelings about the spectral resident of the Masonic Temple. Many other tales have her appearing in the balcony that overlooks the auditorium and at least once in the hallway leading to the room. Over time, more than a few stories of strange encounters in the building have filtered out into the public consciousness. In recent years, these tales have reached the ears of local folklorists, who have taken an active interest in interviewing the witnesses and researching the stories. What they have uncovered is a fascinating catalogue of people who have claimed peculiar experiences at the old structure.

Many of the more recent tales have come from workers and volunteers at the Historical Museum who, on occasion, have been in the building at odd hours of the day and night, sometimes encountering inexplicable incidents. Many have reported the strong sense of a "presence" in the building, not simply in the auditorium section, but in the museum portion of the building as well. At least one witness spoke of coming in early one morning and unlocking the front door, as she was the first one there that day. As she entered the building, however, she noticed a distinct shadow at the top of the stairs leading to the second floor. Quickly, the shadow moved away, as though someone did not wish to be seen. Yet a later search of the upstairs section revealed no human habitation.

Another worker reported an even more direct encounter with an unseen presence in the building. As she related to one researcher, "I used to come into the building to work after I had gotten my kids down for the night. I would go into the computer room, sit at the secretary's counter and work till late at night. I used to hear the usual creeks and moans that you hear in an old building and it never bothered me.

"One night, I was working in that office at the computer with my back to the doorway, and sometime between nine and ten o'clock, I heard footsteps out in the hall. It was clear and distinct and it unnerved me. I knew that I was the only one there and that all the doors were locked, but it was a weird feeling. Suddenly, I was overwhelmed with the feeling that there was someone in the room with me, standing just behind me looking over my shoulder. I realized that the hair on the back of my neck was standing straight up. I didn't know if I should turn around or not, but when I did, there was no one there. However, I absolutely knew that there was someone in that room! Eventually, I did go out into the hall to check and see if there was anyone around, and of course, I was totally alone in the building."

The staff member in question went on to explain that a maintenance worker who knew nothing of her experience that night came to her sometime later and told of a similar experience in the same room. Others have reported hearing running footsteps in the hallways late at night and the unnerving sound of whispering coming from empty rooms.

Perhaps one of the more intriguing and chilling tales has been told by a young woman who served as an intern at the museum several years ago. The woman reported that one day, she left her usual work area on the second floor, where she was employed cataloguing and documenting artifacts. She went to the display area of the museum to put literature in a small box that hangs in the hall, and as she placed the material in the box, she was surprised to find a strange piece of paper already there.

Curious, she glanced at the paper to find a formal billing statement she did not at first recognize. However, her curiosity turned to stunned amazement when, upon closer examination, she realized that she was holding an invoice for her father's funeral. Her father, who had passed away recently, had been buried in another part of the state and she had not seen the bill for his funeral until that moment. Needless to say, she was dumbfounded as to how this bill could have made its way to Franklin and into a literature box at the museum.

Intrigued by the stories, a few years ago two local ghost researchers decided to do some firsthand investigation of the Masonic Temple. Visiting the building alone one evening, the pair felt the strong sense of a presence in a small room just outside the auditorium. This is a place they would later discover would have been used by the Masonic "Guard at Arms," whose job it was to guard the entrance to the area when meetings and rituals were going on inside. She notes that this feeling of presence was accompanied by strong readings from an EMF (Electro Magnetic Fluctuation) meter she had brought along. It is widely held in the paranormal investigation field that such rapid fluctuations in a magnetic field are indicative of paranormal activity in an area.

The pair also reported when leaving the small room outside the auditorium, they left the lights on. Upon returning shortly, they found the lights had been turned off at the switch. Additionally, they both reported a faint aroma of women's perfume in the balcony seating area. Finally, when the pair developed some of the pictures they had taken during their late night tour, they were amazed to find several unaccountable balls of light present on two of the negatives and one picture revealed a seat in the auditorium balcony had been lowered as if a presence was watching the show. Clearly, no strange lights had been noticed when the pictures were taken and photos taken immediately before and after these shots show no such light present.

Throughout the city of Franklin, these fascinating tales are whispered. From a stately Victorian home where the uneasy spirit of a child taken from life before his time is said to still play mischievous pranks, to a ghostly prohibitionist expressing her dismay at her home being turned into a restaurant, to a lady in white treading the halls the Masonic Temple, the tales seem many and varied. Perhaps their presence can be explained by the very charm and ambiance of the city they are said to inhabit.

Walking through the streets of this captivating small Midwestern city, it is easy to imagine that it would be a congenial setting to while away an afterlife. Perhaps this might explain the legion of spectral residents that Franklin claims in its population. They are a part of the lore, the history and the charm of the city and an intriguing part of Indiana ghostlore.

9
GHOSTS OF THE SILVER SCREEN

I know it's hard to believe, son, but this place, this little place, this wasn't a theater then, this was a palace! Any man, woman, child, you, me, it didn't matter, you bought your ticket and you walked in and you...you were in a palace. It was like a dream. It was like heaven, like you died and went to a palace in heaven, that's what it was like. Maybe you had problems and worries out there, but once you came through that door, they didn't matter anymore. In here, you were safe. Maybe it was just an escape from reality, but...oh, god...it was beautiful. I'll tell you, in a place like this, the magic is all around you. All the time. Everywhere. In every thing. The trick...is to see it.

—Michael Sloane, "The Majestic"

Movie houses are places of dreams. Since their inception, movies have taken us from the mundane world in which we sometimes live and transported us to a world of fantasies, nightmares, drama and mystery. Theaters have become our cultural shrines where in the comfortable confines of their dark interiors we are swept away to worlds far removed from our day to day existence. Those building theaters in the great age of American cinema seemed to understand our romantic fascination with the movies and built theaters appropriate to the milieu.

Theaters built in the first half of the twentieth century were designed as places fit for dreams. Ornate and magnificent, these grand palaces of the cinema were an escape for the sometime turbulent times of the era.

Today, movies are most often viewed in the cookie-cutter seats of suburban multiplex theaters. Gone are the dark, cavernous auditoriums and the high, ornate chandeliers. Gone are the rich oriental carpeted aisles leading to upholstered chairs. Gone are the elegance and the otherworldly ambiance of the movie house. The day of the classic American theater has passed and with it has passed some of the charm and mystery of American cinema.

Still, throughout the width and breadth of Indiana, one can find historical movie theaters once more open to the public. From small town, single-screen movie houses to the elegant grand dames of the theater world, some classic movie theaters are emerging once again. And, in at least a few locales, it seems as though some mysterious remnants of their pasts are emerging with them.

Tales of haunted theaters are part of ghostlore from across the globe. When the ghost of Hamlet's father strode across the stage in the first production of Shakespeare's work, he was following in the spectral footsteps of yet more real phantoms already said to tread the boards. A survey of ghostlore from around the world and the United States produces volumes of ghosts said to inhabit the stage.

Perhaps this is only natural owing to the very nature of theaters themselves. Since time immemorial, theaters have always been places of magic and imagination, serving both the social and intellectual needs of their communities. Whether it is the elderly couple coming to relive a portion of their youth, the family enjoying a "night on the town," or the young couple discreetly courting in the back row, theaters are the places where life itself unfolds. Within their walls, large and small, there resides an endless sea of memories of happiness and innocent joys. Further, since it is said that spirits seem particularly disposed to return to the sites of their former happiness, perhaps it is understandable that theaters are also repositories for ghost stories as well.

Despite the widespread knowledge of phantoms in "legitimate" (or live stage production) theaters, movie theaters, from grand palaces in large cities to their small town counterparts, host their share of ghostly activity. Perhaps due to otherworldly snobbery, most specters seem to prefer the company of actors and few seem drawn to the movies. Nevertheless, stories of haunted movie houses do exist. Given the dark, mysterious mood evoked by classic movie houses and the magic that seems to pervade their very atmosphere, "spectral moviegoers" may well feel at home. Perhaps it is that magic that gives life to such ghostly tales.

Indiana can boast of several such theaters. One in particular is a decaying edifice that was once one of the most striking and majestic architectural marvels ever constructed in eastern Indianapolis. Standing today amid the urban sprawl and decay, the Rivoli Theater is a sad reminder of a bygone day. Still, deep within its dust-covered seats and crumbling walls, there lies some remnant of its past glory. Indeed, today a dedicated group of residents is working to restore this great lady to the grandeur she once displayed.

If the whispered tales of the place are true, it seems that some part of its vaunted past may already be residing within its walls. For, as the dark streaks of night gather in the eastern sky, it is said that along the dusty aisles of the Rivoli, the dead walk with silent tread. Perhaps like the theater itself, they are searching for the glory they had in life.

The Rivoli was first constructed in the halcyon days of the American theater, the 1920s. The "roaring twenties" was a time of great exuberance in America. From clandestine speakeasies distributing forbidden spirits to Americans longing for the healing grape to popular (and sometimes bawdy) dance contests, America was hungry for entertainment. In such an environment, the advent of moving pictures was a godsend for a nation still recovering from the horrors of World War I.

To feed this hunger for entertainment, major movie studios churned out endless reels featuring the likes of Buster Keaton and Greta Garbo. In order to profit from both the production and distribution of these movies, studios began to build theaters all across the nation from humble, local movie houses to grand, imposing edifices that graced larger cities.

Universal Pictures, the largest and most aggressive of the major studios, built 315 such movie houses across the United States and the Rivoli Theater was one of its most ambitious projects. No less a personage than movie mogul Carl Laemmle Jr., president of Universal Pictures, had a hand in its design, commissioning architect Henry Ziegler Dietz to create a setting worthy of his plans to dominate the theater business in the United States. His instructions were to plan a theater that was "large, safe, practical and would stand for a long time to serve the community and provide the best the motion picture industry had to offer."

Though these instructions seem a bit prosaic, it can be seen from the fruit they bore that the vision of Laemmle was much grander and more sweeping. The edifice Dietz produced for him was a stunning example of all that a theater could be and seemed to capture the optimism and exuberance of the age itself.

The Rivoli was built in 1927, in the Spanish Mission style. No expense was spared in the construction, which included Indiana limestone, fine sweet gum woodworking, leaded glass windows with copper sashes and solid brass door fittings. The floors, inside and out, were made of Georgia white and Riviera black terrazzo. Ivory lavatory fixtures lavished the patrons in luxury. The theater décor, although not as ornate as some theater palaces, included decorative plastered egg-and-dart molding adorning the walls, a tulip patterned border edging the large domed ceiling and intricate wooden and plaster grillwork fronting the two organ chambers near stage right and stage left. It is said that the dome in the auditorium had small lights that flickered to resemble starlight. The front of the theater building hosted four storefronts that originally included an ice cream parlor named "The Rivoli Tostee Shop."

Built to accommodate 1500 patrons in a single seating, The Rivoli was one of the largest neighborhood theaters in the United States. Pains were taken to make every element of the theater experience ideal for patrons, from the ornate decorations found in the lavatories to the extraordinary acoustics in the auditorium. So flawless was the sound reproduction in the seating section that the famed organist, Desa Byrd, twice recorded albums at the venue.

At its grand opening, Carl Leammle declared the Rivoli "the home of happiness." For the next several years, it lived up to its promise and thousands of Indianapolis residents found the Rivoli a place of dreams.

Still, even grand dreams sometimes come to an end. Sadly, the golden age of the Rivoli Theater lasted just a decade. Two elements caused the doom of the Rivoli, at least in its original incarnation. The first was the Great Depression that swept through the country like a tidal wave during the 1930s. While most Americans eked out economic survival with bare necessities, there was little means left for frills such as entertainment. Attendance at theaters plummeted and though many small movie houses with low overhead costs managed to survive, most of the palatial metropolitan theaters found themselves in dire financial straits.

Ironically, the other fact to spell the end of such grand dames of the movie house industry was the very nature of the industry itself. By the late 1930s, the entertainment industry was being reshaped by the advent of a new and revolutionary development, "talking pictures." Originally dismissed by studio executives as merely a passing fad, this new technology had caught on like a whirlwind with the public.

Studios quickly began scrambling to refit their theaters with sound equipment. In many smaller theaters, the modifications needed were simple enough but in the case of the Rivoli, once again, it was the very grand scale of the theater that worked against it. In a theater of its size, the conversion of the theater to accommodate sound was too expensive for the already financially strapped Universal Pictures to afford. In 1937 the theater was sold.

Eventually, the owners refitted the theater to accommodate sound pictures, but it would never return to its former glory. Over the coming decades, the Rivoli would pass through a series of owners, its beauty slowly fading with the passing years. Still, the theater continued to provide the east side of Indianapolis with a venue for entertainment. In addition to the countless movies shown there, the venerable stage hosted many live performances ranging from Gloria Swanson to Linda Ronstadt.

In 1976, Charles Richard Chulchian purchased the Rivoli, which was already in a sad state of disrepair. Although Mr. Chulchian managed to keep the theater operations going for nearly twenty years, the fate of the old theater seemed set. In February 1992, the Rivoli closed its doors, apparently for the last time. With its passing, a classic era of entertainment in central Indiana came to an end as well.

Today, the theater stands dark and dismal amid the onrush of urban life. However, when one glances through the clouded front windows into the lobby, it is not hard to imagine the majesty that once was this house of dreams. A rusty suit of armor adorns one side of the lobby and the once ornamental woodwork and grand furnishings are now covered with a thick coating of plaster dust from the crumbling ceiling. The walls are still decked with faded movie posters from years gone by and the concessions area now stands unmanned and silent. Inside the main auditorium, one is at once struck by the huge expanse of the place and the dreary atmosphere that pervades the decaying structure. Here, too, the once colorful carpeting and plush seats are covered with the debris of a crumbling ceiling.

Through the ceiling itself, once so painstakingly painted to resemble starlight, holes now allow a glimpse of the true night sky. All around is an aura of bygone glory and gloomy neglect. It is an effect that is at once solemn and somehow otherworldly. Perhaps it is not so surprising, then, that in such a setting spirits are said to roam. Amidst the ambiance of faded splendor and deathly stillness, where once magic and laughter reigned, phantoms of the past linger amid the dust.

photo courtesy of Mark Marimen

The lobby of the Rivoli Theater

photo courtesy of Mark Marimen

The lobby of the Rivoli Theater

Due to the long history of the Rivoli, the origins of these spectral patrons are impossible to trace. When Charles Chulchian purchased the Rivoli in 1976, the theater had already garnered a quiet reputation in the neighborhood for being haunted. Previous owners related to Mr. Chulchian incidents of coming to open the theater early in the day, only to find two people already sitting in the auditorium. As the owners approached the couple to ask them how they had gotten in, they were bewildered to see the figures fade away before their very eyes.

At first, Charles says that he tended to laugh off the tales as incidents of an over-active imagination. However, before long he began to question his safe assumption. Soon after taking on the role of owner and manager of the theater, Mr. Chulchian became aware of other seemingly inexplicable tales centered around the place. One of these incidents came to light when two patrons, coming in for an afternoon movie, entered the theater to find that they were not the first ones in the auditorium. While this was hardly noteworthy, upon inspection there was something about their fellow patrons that stuck them as decidedly odd.

As they later described the scene to Mr. Chulchian, upon coming into the theater, they noticed a man and woman seated toward the front of the auditorium. The man was dressed in a tuxedo and the woman wore a long, formal evening gown. As though this alone was not enough to shock the onlookers, what made the pair particularly eerie was the fact that they sat silently, staring at the dark screen intently, presumably enjoying a movie that had ended years before.

Hastily exiting the auditorium, the startled patrons sought out Charles Chulchian and quizzed him with regard to the strange couple. Puzzled, he explained to them that they were the first customers of the day and definitely should be the only other people in the building. Together they entered the auditorium to find it apparently vacant.

Although certainly disquieting, tales of these "non-paying customers" were not the end of the stories told of the Rivoli Theater. Over the years an amazing number of peculiar stories have been related to this venerable house of dreams. Most might well have passed out of remembrance, if not for the efforts of amateur historian and ghost researcher Kathy Harlow, who has not simply taken an active interest in the ghosts of the Rivoli but in the theater itself and who is playing a vital role in the planned renovation of the theater. It is through her tireless efforts that both the building and the ghostly tales told of it have been preserved.

According to Ms. Harlow, the spectral encounters at the Rivoli were not limited to the main auditorium of the building. Female patrons repeatedly reported strange events in the ladies' vanity room just off the lobby. More than a few reported an uncomfortable feeling of presence in the room, as though they were being watched by an unseen manifestation. Others reported commodes flushing in empty stalls and at least one told of watching, horrified, as the handles of the sink turned on and off for no apparent reason.

On at least one occasion, apparently the presence in the bathroom was not content to remain unseen. One moviegoer reported coming into the bathroom and standing before the sink freshening her makeup. As she gazed intently into the mirror, she saw the door to one of the facilities open and a woman emerge. A little surprised, since she had assumed that she was alone in the room, she quickly turned toward the woman to speak to her, but when she turned, she found the room empty. The woman had simply vanished.

In speaking to Charles Chulchian, Ms. Harlow discovered that in the first few years of his ownership of the Rivoli, he had difficulty in keeping employees. Workers reported seeing buckets and cleaning supplies move across rooms of their own volition. Somewhat more ominously, some reported being shoved from behind by unseen hands. Understandably, such employees rarely stayed long at their jobs.

Those who did choose to stay refused to clean the auditorium alone, reporting an overwhelming feeling of being watched. Nor were they alone in sensing something otherworldly within the walls of the Rivoli. Once, while Mr. Chulchian and fellow workers watched, a faucet in a utility closet turned on and off by itself. Enigmatic figures have been reported throughout the building. Mr. Chulchian reports a friend encountering the spectral figure of a woman on the stairs leading to the projection booth. Others too have caught a glimpse of a female form in the Rivoli and over the years she has acquired the nickname "Lady Rivoli."

If, indeed, Lady Rivoli walks the darkened expanse of the theater, she has become a fixture there. Moreover, she has been known to be fiercely protective of her home and its contents. Ms. Harlow found this out in a rather dramatic fashion on one occasion when she received a memoir of the Rivoli from Mr. Chulchian.

"After admiring the wrought iron chandelier that hung in the women's powder room at the Rivoli," she now recalls, "Mr. Chulchian presented the chandelier to me as a gift and I took it and hung it at home."

"One evening, soon after, Mr. Chulchian visited my home. While we were sitting on my back porch, we heard a loud crackling sound, like electricity popping, emanating from the side of the house. After ignoring three episodes of this sound, we heard a large bang as though someone took two metal trash cans and crashed them together."

"We sprang from our seats to find nothing disturbed," she continues. "Since I didn't have metal trash cans, we could not understand what made that sound. However, as we further investigated, we found that a large brick had been thrown into the bed of my new, white pickup truck. The brick hit so hard it was pulverized into powder. We could not explain how the brick did no damage to the truck, not a scratch, yet hit so hard it almost disintegrated. We also could not explain the electrical popping sound." Later that night, after returning to the theater, Mr. Chulchian heard a female voice demand the return of the chandelier. The gift was returned and Kathy experienced no further disturbances at her home. The chandelier, once again, hangs at the Rivoli.

Not only has Lady Rivoli reportedly interceded for her adopted home, but for Mr. Chulchian himself, perhaps because he loves the theater as much as she seems to. Evidence of her feelings comes from many incidents. The first occurred several years ago when Charles, tireless in his efforts to maintain the decaying structure, was working on the boiler in the early hours of the morning.

According to the story he related to Ms. Harlow, he had bent to work on the old boiler when he became aware of a feeling of intense cold in the room. After a moment, he distinctly felt two very cold feminine arms wrap around him from behind. According to the story he told Kathy, he quickly stood and turned around, only to find himself alone. Uncharacteristically (yet understandably) giving in to fear, Charles reports running from the boiler room, up two flights of stairs and through the massive auditorium to the projection booth, turning on every available light along the way.

Another dramatic tale that seems to indicate Lady Rivoli's benevolence toward Mr. Chulchian occurred more recently and might well have saved his life. In the spring of 2002, as a part of his ongoing quest to save the Rivoli, Charles, accompanied by Kathy Harlow and two other gentlemen, was on the roof in order to get a bid on replacing it. As Mr. Chulchian walked to the middle of the roof over the auditorium, Ms. Harlow and the two roofing contractors were horrified to see the roof suddenly give way and Charles disappear into the black void below.

Momentarily paralyzed at the sight of her dear friend apparently falling to his death eighty-five feet below, Ms. Harlow stood motionless. However, after a moment that seemed like an eternity, Ms. Harlow and the two men were shocked and relieved to see Mr. Chulchian's head emerge from the hole, calmly assuring them that he was all right. Carefully, the three extricated him from the hole and took him downstairs.

There he explained that as the roof gave way beneath him, he felt himself falling helplessly through space for one terrible moment. Then, as he fell, he physically felt someone pushing his body sideways and over one of the supporting beams a few feet below and to one side of the place where the roof collapsed. He landed unhurt but unable to explain, by any logical means, how his falling body had been moved to save his life. Perhaps, as he and Kathy later surmised, Lady Rivoli had taken a hand in saving the man who is so intent on saving her home.

Reports of strange phenomena at the Rivoli have ranged from the bizarre to the merely mischievous. From his living quarters in the upstairs section of the Rivoli, Charles has reported objects disappearing only to be found later in odd locations. On one occasion, an eyeglass holder disappeared from a drawer where it was always kept. Three days later the case suddenly appeared in the middle of his living room floor, only minutes after he had walked through the room. Batteries have vanished from his apartment, only to be found later in a separate apartment on the opposite side of the building.

Kathy Harlow relates another tale that began one day when Charles mentioned he had been unable to find his cell phone, which had disappeared from a dresser drawer in his apartment several days earlier. "While sitting in the projection booth alone, I spoke out loud to the Lady Rivoli and told her that if she knew where the phone was, it would be appreciated if she would let us know," she says. "It seems that Lady Rivoli answered my request. The next morning when I woke, I was astounded to find Charlie's cell phone lying on the nightstand next to my bed."

Lady Rivoli has made herself felt by a variety of means over the years. As has been noted, on rare occasions she has also been glimpsed and at least once, her presence may have been caught on camera. Recently, Charles and a friend decided to experiment with an infrared camera aimed toward the auditorium early one morning. As Kathy explains, "The infrared camera was set up and was on, but there was no tape. Charlie and his friend watched the phenomenon in the viewfinder of the camera as it happened, at about 3:00 A.M."

As Kathy describes the tale told to her by Charles, at exactly 2:58 A.M., the camera picked up a light suddenly appearing behind a seat in the auditorium. The light grew in intensity until it formed the approximate size and shape of a human being. Then, the light moved to the left of the camera screen and, at exactly 3:02 A.M., disappeared.

Interestingly, this is not the only time that the phantoms of the Rivoli have been caught on camera. As Ms. Harlow reports, "A recent photo taken by a guest while I was giving a tour of the Rivoli may have revealed the phantom man and woman that have been seen over the years by patrons. The guest took a picture into the auditorium from the middle of the stage. What appeared in the picture was unnerving. As seen by many patrons over the years, there was a vague outline of a spectral man in a black top hat and a spectral woman in a white dress sitting side by side on auditorium left, three rows from the front. What was surprising was that they were accompanied by the vague outline of a spectral child, which was standing in the front row. Apparently, the phantoms are forever being entertained by Hollywood's finest, or were we the show?"

Even today, strange events continue to occur regularly at the Rivoli. Inside doors have been known to lock of their own volition. Lights frequently turn on and off by themselves, light bulbs explode as visitors walk by and objects continue to disappear. As the activity escalates in the building during preparation for renovation, unexplained events seem to be increasing in recent months.

Today, thanks to the efforts of Kathy Harlow and the Rivoli Theater & Concert Hall Inc., new life may be returning to the venerable old structure. In 2004, the Rivoli received designation as a National Historic Landmark and plans are underway to renovate and restore the theater to its former glory. Soon, perhaps, the Rivoli will rise once more, resplendent and beautiful from years of neglect and decay.

This may well please Lady Rivoli, who still makes her presence known on a nearly daily basis there. In the end, perhaps the Rivoli belongs to her and to whatever other phantoms walk the dark halls as much as it belongs to anyone. For as darkness falls on this vaunted theater, it is said that spirits walk once more, perhaps searching for a past that has long since faded into the mist of time.

10
THE RESURRECTIONISTS RETURN

The night of February 24th, 1890, was a wild one. The skies above New Albany were painted with bright flashes of lightning, while thunder rolled ominously all around. Rain fell in ragged sheets blown by a cold wind that swept through the Old North Cemetery, slowly numbing the hands of those who crouched, waiting expectantly among the tombstones. It was, as events turned out, a perfect night for the macabre story about to unfold.

As the midnight hour arrived, the fury of the storm was at its height. Lightning split the sky overhead, momentarily turning the night into day, then just as quickly, plunged it back into gloomy darkness. In the light of one of those flashes, the sight of a horse-drawn wagon could be seen proceeding down Eighth Street, over a small bridge and slowly, almost leisurely, coming to a stop at the cemetery gate. The resurrectionists had arrived.

The driver alighted and hitched his team to the cemetery fence. Now joined by three men who emerged from the recesses of the carriage, the group warily entered the cemetery grounds, their every sense on edge. The tallest member of the group took the lead with a shuttered lantern. It was he who knew the location of the prizes they sought. His companions straggled behind bearing the implements of their trade—two spades, a pry pole and hatchet. After a moment's hesitation, their leader found his bearings and then directed them to the grave of Tom Johnson, who had been buried just a few days previously.

Arriving at the gentle mound of the new grave, two members of the ghoulish team were about to put shovel to earth when suddenly a shout from a few yards away broke over the roar of the wind. "Put your hands up!" Instantly, the group broke and ran in different directions. One, younger and bolder than his companions, turned in the direction of the challenge, his hand reaching for the revolver in his pocket. As he did so, a series of shots rang out above the storm's fury. His body shuddered for a moment, and then he seemed to collect himself and turned toward the men quickly approaching out of the darkness, his hands raised in surrender. In another moment, however, he pitched forward into the wet dirt. The single volley had placed a bullet through his heart.

Two of his compatriots were quickly apprehended but a third was more fortunate, having quickly scaled the northern wall and regained the carriage, which was soon flying back down Eighth Street and on into the wild night. Now more law enforcement officials appeared from a different direction and, hurriedly securing their prisoners, marched them through the rain to the New Albany jail. The entire episode had taken little more than fifteen minutes to unfold, and owing to the violent storm and the lateness of the hour, few local citizens were aware of it at the time. However as the morning light washed over the town, so also did the ominous news: New Albany had narrowly escaped the horror of being visited by graver robbers once again.

The practice of grave robbing brings to mind scenes from a hundred old horror films. Dark, stormy nights and a taciturn physician in the company of a sinister assistant form the plots of a score of old monster movies, since the image was penned by Mary Shelley in her immortal work *Frankenstein*. However, it should be noted that the actual practice of body snatching predated Shelley's work by many years. Further, while there may be some similarities in the actual setting and practice of grave robbing, as noted above, the true intent of its practitioners was much different from Shelley's ill fated hero.

While the practice of grave robbing dates back centuries, its modern history began with the rise of formal medical education in the late eighteenth century. Prior to that point, the training of medical professionals was pursued as an apprenticeship process, young doctors learning their trade from observing a seasoned physician. By the last decades of the 1700s, however, more formal medical schools began to spring up, primarily in the large cities of Europe.

Now, for the first time, students were formally taught in classes by trained instructors. Though the curriculum did vary from school to school, it became accepted that one of the necessary components of medical education was a sound understanding of human anatomy. Further, it quickly became apparent that for students to truly understand the nature and structure of the human body there could be no substitute for firsthand experience in observing its complexities.

As distasteful as it may seem to the population in general, this quest for anatomical knowledge could only be fulfilled by allowing students to at least observe, if not actually participate in, the dissection of a human cadaver. While the practice of human dissection for medical education has become a common practice in medical schools today, it was considered far from acceptable in eighteenth century society.

A large part of the opposition to human dissection came from the church, some segments of which believed that a body must be kept whole after death in order to be resurrected by God into the afterlife. While this notion is no longer considered part of most Christian teaching, the threat of losing one's salvation and entrance to Heaven was a strong deterrent to the practice of dissection in the minds of the common people of the time.

During the first years of the eighteenth century, the meager supply of cadavers available to medical schools came chiefly from the penal systems of their respective countries. Often, the criminal codes included dissection of the corpses of executed felons as a part of the penalty for the crime they had committed. This was considered a strong deterrent to crime, being considered a fate worse than death itself. Indeed, this penalty was sometimes thwarted by the families of those executed, who were known to bribe corrupt officials to release the body to them, or at times even steal the deceased from the gallows before they could be delivered to the local medical school for dissection.

As medical schools began to grow and flourish, it became apparent that this meager trickle of corpses available for dissection was inadequate. Medical education practices prescribed that one cadaver was necessary for every six students, and the number of students enrolling was quickly growing. Clearly, another source needed to be found if new doctors were to properly learn their craft. Soon, out of desperation or perhaps mere convenience, doctors turned to a more macabre and grisly source: the graves of the newly deceased.

By 1770, grave robbing was a common, if illicit part of medical education. In some cases, ruffians within the community were paid to desecrate the graves of those who had been recently buried and deliver their bodies to the medical schools. Commonly called "sack'em up men" (or, more benignly "resurrectionists"), they plied their trade for many years throughout Europe.

However, grave robbing was not reserved simply for hired thieves and scoundrels. Quite often, it was the medical students and teachers themselves who journeyed by night to deserted graveyards, only to return a few hours later bearing a cold, limp sack. This practice seems to have been particularly prevalent in Scotland, which was a center of medical education at the time. Some medical schools in Scotland were even known to charge a set number of cadavers as a part of the students' tuition. Students who refused to do the grave robbing, or to hire others to do so for them, were fined and even expelled from the schools in question. So frequent was the practice in Scotland that a folk song from the era proclaimed, *"There is not a churchyard in our fair land that has not felt the touch of the sack'em up's hand."*

Interestingly, it was not only medical students who needed cadavers for dissection. Sometimes established physicians were known to rob graves for their purposes as well. As physician and medical historian Dr.

courtesy of Culver Prints, Inc.

Nineteenth century print of "Ms. Cassell being dragged from her grave in Indianapolis by embryo Doctors."

Douglas Zale notes, "At the time, there were no medical specialties. A common doctor would regularly find himself doing surgery on his patients. If you were that doctor and needed to learn how to do a comparatively simple operation such as an appendectomy, you had two choices. You could either experiment on a live patient and take your chances, or you could acquire a cadaver and practice removing the appendix from a patient whose health you would not adversely affect."

Thus, it can be seen that as horrific and distasteful as the practice of grave robbing may be to modern sensibilities, it did serve a necessary and even beneficial function. When the first medical school in America was established in Philadelphia in 1765, grave robbing came to this continent. Understandably, it proved no more popular in the colonies than it had in Europe. While, amazingly, it was not until 1789 that the first law was passed making it a crime to steal a body, long before then public outrage at the practice frequently led to violence. In 1788 outraged citizens of New York City precipitated a riot while ransacking the rooms of anatomy students and professors at Columbia College Medical School in search of bodies. Similar incidents were recorded in Philadelphia and in Camden, New Jersey.

While grave robbing was never an epidemic in Indiana, the state was not completely spared of the grisly ritual. A print widely distributed in periodicals of the time shows the grave of a young girl being desecrated in Indianapolis, presumably for use in the Indiana Medical School, which was housed in the city.

In the New Albany incident, the crime was an interstate affair. It began earlier in the day when Dr. J.T. Blackburn, a physician from nearby Louisville, Kentucky, left his office to journey across the Ohio River to New Albany. Blackburn, in addition to being a respected practicing physician in Louisville, was also Chief Demonstrator of Anatomy at the Kentucky School of Medicine there. Later, it would become evident that in this capacity he was in charge of acquiring cadavers for dissection in medical training.

On that day, Dr. Blackburn had come to New Albany in search of information of a most particular kind. He located the Old North Cemetery with little trouble, possibly having been there on previous occasions. Arriving, he found a young man, William Peebles, working as assistant to the groundskeeper. After a few moments, their conversation took an ominous turn when the physician offered the young man $2.00 to show him the graves of two local men, Thomas Johnson and Edward Pearce, who had been buried there within the last few days. His suspicions aroused by this mysterious visitor, Peebles at first refused, but his scruples seemed to be allayed when the bribe was increased to $20.00, an astronomical sum in those days. After Peebles led him to the graves in question his anonymous visitor took his leave, cautioning the worker to remain silent as to their transaction.

Mr. Peebles had no intention of keeping the strange visit a secret. According to newspaper accounts of the day, no sooner had the physician left in the direction of Louisville than the young man was on his way to Cemetery Sexton Dan Shrader to tell his tale. Recognizing this contact as a prelude to grave robbery, Shrader then went to New Albany Mayor John McDonald, who in turn sent him to Chief of Police John Stonecipher.

Since the Old North Cemetery had been the site of past grave robberies, which were attributed to medical students from Louisville, the Chief immediately set to work to capture the ghoulish thieves. He quickly enlisted the help of two trusted officers, Michael Hennessy and Tom Cannon to set a trap. That night the officers, along with local citizens Jack and Jim Johnson (brothers to Thomas Johnson, whose body was one of the intended prizes in the raid) and Elmer Hopper went to Old North Cemetery to put a stop to the macabre desecrations.

The group entered the graveyard shortly after dark and divided into two teams, each hiding near one of the graves in question. With the weather providing a dramatic and perhaps apropos setting for the escapade, the teams waited for hours through the blinding rain and wild winds for the arrival of the grave robbers. As the midnight hour passed, their patience was rewarded by the arrival of a horse-drawn buggy bearing Dr. Blackburn and Dr. W.E. Grant, as well as two hired assistants.

As the *Louisville Post* recounted the events that next day, "Hardly a soul was abroad when the awful stillness of the cemetery was broken by the sound of wheels…The wagon stopped at the gate. The occupants alighted, leaving their team hitched to the fence and came into the cemetery. The watchers, alert to every sound, had concealed themselves, and the grave robbers passed the first division and proceeded to the Johnson grave. They had barely reached it when the Johnson boys and their friends called out, 'Throw up your hands!'"

The Johnson brothers had acted quickly, perhaps too quickly as events were to turn out. When the incident was over, two men were in custody, one had escaped—never to be apprehended—and one lay dead, his life's blood slowly seeping into the grass of the cemetery.

Quickly, the captured men were tied and then marched to the New Albany jail. As has been noted, so wild was the night and so late the hour that no public notice was made of the arrest at the time. By the next morning however, the news had spread throughout the community and an angry mob had gathered outside the jail, demanding vigilante justice. By mid morning, as the prisoners were transported to the county courthouse for arraignment, the mob had grown to several hundred. That morning, all three of the defendants were arraigned, charged with grave desecration, a crime that could carry a prison term of several years. Additionally, for the physicians involved, a conviction could lead to the permanent loss of their medical licenses.

Before any trial could begin, however, a spirited debate erupted between the citizens of Louisville and their Hoosier neighbors. Vitriolic letters and editorials appeared in Kentucky newspapers demanding the release of the doctors. One editorial even went so far as to suggest that the governor of Kentucky mount a military raid into Indiana to force their liberation. This in turn led to calls in the *New Albany Ledger* for citizens to prepare an armed defense of their state.

Meanwhile, the legal case against the defendants began to be questioned as well. As strange as it now seems, a great many grave robbers in that day and age were never prosecuted for their crimes, even if apprehended. Many states did not have laws against body snatching, while others declared that a cadaver was not property and thus could not be stolen. While, at the time, there was an Indiana statute declaring grave desecration a crime, the question in this case was whether or not that crime had actually been committed.

Newspaper accounts from the time presented contradictory reports as to whether or not any dirt had actually been shoveled from the grave of Thomas Johnson. Some indicated that about half a bushel basket of earth had been removed, while the majority indicated that the prospective grave robbers had been ambushed before the first shovel had touched the earth. Some questioned whether the simple intent to commit a crime was enough to secure a conviction. In any case, it is clear that reasonable doubt could be raised as to whether or not the charge of grave robbery could be sustained against the three prisoners. However, in the highly charged atmosphere of New Albany, legal technicalities probably mattered little to the local citizens at the time.

Disappointingly, the ultimate fate of the doctors and their accomplices is not known. Newspaper accounts report that they were released on bond several days after their arrest pending trial, but the results of that trial, if it even occurred, have been lost to the mists of history. As was noted in a 1958 *New Albany Ledger-Tribune* summary of the case, "The case made its leisurely way through court procedure and by the time of its disposal there apparently wasn't enough interest in the matter to merit an item in the public press..."

In truth, a review of press clippings from the time reveals no notice of the outcome of the case against Doctors Blackburn and Grant as well as their hired assistant. Further, legal records from the 1800s are not readily available for public inspection. Clearly, the legal conclusion of this case cannot be known. Nevertheless, if the stories told in and around Old North Cemetery are true, there may well be repercussions from this case that still may echo to this day. Far from a simple verdict culled from yellowed newspapers or official court transcripts, these are inexplicable reverberations from a macabre and grisly crime.

While the fate of Dr. Blackburn and Dr. Grant may never be known, what is clear is that while the pair whiled away their time in a county jail in New Albany, George Brown was being laid in a humble grave in Louisville. Brown, who was a custodial worker at the Kentucky School of Medicine, had been hired by Dr. Blackburn to assist him on that fateful night and had paid for the adventure with his life. While the public furor over the doctors' actions raged, the life and death of George Brown were largely forgotten. With little public fanfare, his body was lowered into an anonymous grave.

However, there are some in the area of New Albany who believe Mr. Brown has not lain quiet in his nameless grave. Throughout the ensuing century, strange tales began to circulate around the area suggesting that this is one resurrectionist who has refused to stay dead and forgotten.

According to an article in the *Indiana Folklore Journal* from the mid 1970s, many tales have been whispered regarding strange goings-on in and around the Old North Cemetery. Although the cemetery is still active, having grown and expanded through the years, the tales center on the oldest section, where the graves of Thomas Johnson and Edward

Pearce are found. Visitors to the cemetery, particularly in the evening hours, have reported seeing strange forms moving among the tombstones. Vincent Madden, who grew up just a few miles from the cemetery, remembers one such incident that occurred several years ago.

"It was in the early '70s," he now remembers, "and a couple of us guys were out driving around on a beautiful summer evening. For some reason I cannot now recall, we decided to cruise through the cemetery. It was close to closing time and the place was pretty much empty, but as we were driving past the old section, one of my buddies pointed out the window and said 'Check out that weird looking guy!'

"The driver hit the brakes and I looked out the window and there, standing among the tombstones, was this young black man dressed in what they used to call a greatcoat. It was strange enough to see someone dressed that heavily on a warm summer night, but this coat looked like it was from some old movie. I remember he also had a hat that he had pulled down almost over his eyes. We all just stopped and kind of stared, but he didn't appear to notice us. Instead, he seemed to wander among the tombstones and then, all of a sudden, he sort of faded away. It was like one minute he was there and the next he was gone. We just stared at one another for a long instant and then someone yelled 'Let's get out of here, man!' and let me tell you, we did."

As strange as this account may seem, it is not the only report of strange activities in and around the Old North Cemetery. Deanna Roberts Morton,* who currently lives in Evansville, is a widow whose late husband worked part-time there in the 1950s. According to the stories her husband told her, other workers occasionally spoke of strange incidents that were said to have occurred there.

"My husband worked at the cemetery for a number of years, and he became close friends with some of the old-time workers there," she explains. "One day when he was working with one of the guys in one of the oldest sections, this old guy pointed out a couple of graves and said that a grave robber had been killed there way, way back, before the turn of the century.

"He then went on to say that workers had long said they did not like to work in that section of the cemetery, particularly alone. There was a weird feeling about that section. He added that a night watchman had actually called the police when he had driven past that section and seen a figure or figures moving in the darkness right around those tombstones. Then, he swore he heard a shot followed by the thud of a body. When the police arrived, they found no one around."

Perhaps it might be possible to attribute these incidents to overactive imaginations or even the strange tricks that night can play on the eyes. However, taken together they begin to suggest an inexplicable pattern of reports that center around the cemetery. Most seem to happen in the oldest section, but another sighting came just outside the gates one night in the 1960s. It is told by Mark Rhine, who remembers a fateful trip past the cemetery with his parents late one night. "I was about ten or eleven years old, and I was with my parents on the way back from visiting my aunt in New Albany," he recalls. "The people in my father's family were all night people and sometimes the family gatherings would go late, so it was almost midnight when we started on our way home to Terre Haute. I was sitting in the back seat, and I remember it had started to rain hard. Dad was talking to me about growing up in New Albany, and he mentioned that we were coming up on the old cemetery.

"I was getting drowsy, I think, and was probably not paying much attention, but in a second, he slowed down, and then I heard my mom say, 'What's that doing there?' I sat up and looked out the window, and through the rain I saw a big black shape along the side of the road, next to the fence. I strained my eyes and when we passed, I could see that it was an old-fashioned horse and buggy. I know it sounds crazy—heck it even seemed crazy to me at the time, but it was there, big as life, and then in a second we were past it.

"That might have been the end of it," Mark continues, "but my mother could not get over what we had just seen. As we drove down the road, she couldn't stop trying to figure out what a horse and buggy would be doing tied up at the cemetery at that hour of the night. After about a mile, she actually convinced my dad to turn around and go back to see if someone needed help. We got back to the spot where we had seen the buggy, but now it was gone. We knew that it had been right there, but now, just a few minutes later, it had vanished. We drove on for about a mile but there was no horse and buggy on the road."

By now totally perplexed, Mark's father turned the car once again, arriving for a third time at the spot where they had seen the phantom buggy. So sure was Mr. Rhine of what he had seen that at his wife's suggestion, he pulled their car over to the side and got out in the rain to examine the area next to the cemetery fence where they had seen the buggy. After several moments he returned to the car and reported that despite the fact that the dirt was soft, no marks of wheels could be found. The buggy, like the other figures that have been noted around the cemetery over the years, had faded with the night.

Today, the former Old North Cemetery (which has been renamed Fairview Cemetery) is a modern, expansive enterprise. Its picturesque grounds provide a beautiful setting to memorialize the lives of those interred there. However, beneath this pastoral landscape there lie hints of a macabre event that shook an entire community over a century ago. Moreover, if the whispered tales are true, it is an event that continues to have inexplicable repercussions even today. Perhaps, in the end, the events that began on a stormy night in February of 1890 are nothing more than a curious historical footnote. However, driving through the former Old North Cemetery on a cool evening, one might well wonder if perhaps the unquiet spirit of a resurrectionist still wanders these hallowed grounds. His is a macabre legend and a somewhat gruesome part of Indiana ghostlore.

EPILOGUE

In the fall of 1996, a letter arrived on my desk one morning from a publishing house called Thunder Bay Press. It was a letter that I had no idea was coming, and yet it would change my life. I had been collecting Indiana ghost stories for some time as a hobby, and about six months earlier had sent them to a friend who wrote professionally to "tell me what she thought." When I had not heard from her in some time, my worst suspicions seemed confirmed—she hated them, and was simply being too kind to write back and say so. What I did not know was that she had forwarded them to Thunder Bay, who was at the time looking to publish regional ghost stories. Their letter informed me that they were interesting in publishing a book I never knew I was writing, and asked me to forward to them the remainder of the stories, which I had never written.

What followed has been nine years riding a whirlwind. Through my wonderful association with Thunder Bay, *Haunted Indiana I* was followed by four more books, the most recent of which you hold in your hands.

During these last nine years, I have always held it to be an honor and a privilege to share the stories told to me from across the Hoosier State with you, my readers. In honesty, I am still swept away with a thrill of delighted surprise when someone says, "I read your books!" Let me thank you for sharing this journey. It truly is a privilege to share with you stories that still awaken the magic and wonder of the world in me. If these stories have entertained you, I am grateful. If they have chilled you (as they have me as I have collected and written them), then I am delighted.

Thanks for sharing these stories with me. Perhaps we may yet share the wonder and chill of other stories on other starlit nights in the future. It is to you, the reader, that I owe my greatest gratitude, and it is my hope that you have enjoyed the last nine years of my work. It has not always been easy or even sane, but it has been a great experience. Thanks for blessing me with your support. In the words of the Grateful Dead, "What a long, strange trip it's been!"

Mark Marimen
May 10, 2005

CREDITS AND SOURCES

Chapter 1: ***"A Grandfather's Tale"***

Mark Marimen, personal research and interviews.

Chapter 2: ***"The Ghosts Of Story"***

Mark Marimen, personal research and interviews.

"The Story Inn" <http.www.storyinn.com>

Chapter 3: ***"The House Call"***

Mark Marimen, personal research and interviews.

Chapter 4: ***"The Return of the Black Widow"***

Mark Marimen, personal research and interviews.

The Mistress of Murder Hill: The Serial Killings of Belle Gunness, Sylvia Elizabeth Shepherd. 2001, "Authorhouse."

"The Legend of Belle Gunness," <http.www.lapcat/belle.html>

"Belle Gunness," Joseph Geringer, <http://www.crimelibrary.com/serial_killers/history/gunness/index_1.html>

"Mystic Indiana" Video, Don and Laura Bernachi, Paz Productions, 2000.

Chapter 5: ***"The Spirits Of The Old County Jail"***

Mark Marimen, personal research and interviews.

"Mystic Indiana" Video, Don and Laura Bernachi, Paz Productions, 2000.

Chapter 6: ***"The Wistful Spirits of Tuckaway"***

Mark Marimen, personal research and interviews.

American Bungalow magazine, Spring 2005.

The Ghostly Gazetteer, Arthur Myers, Contemporary Books, 1990.

"Mrs. George Phillip Meier Honored by Tribune," *The Indianapolis Sunday Star,* April 2, 1944.

Chapter 7: ***"A Ghost on the Beat"***

Mark Marimen, personal research and interviews.

Chapter 8: ***"The Ghostly Guests of Franklin"***

Mark Marimen, personal research and interviews.

Kathy Harlow, personal research and interviews.

"The Murder At Franklin College," Gerry Marie Till, *Indiana Folklore Journal*, Fall 1975.

"The Place To Be," Scott Hall, *The Daily Journal Online*, February 14, 2005.

Chapter 9: ***"The Ghosts of the Silver Screen"***

Mark Marimen, personal research and interviews.

Kathy Harlow, personal research and interviews.

Chapter 10: ***"The Resurrectionists Return"***

Mark Marimen, personal research and interviews.

Body Snatching, Suzanne M. Shultz, McFarland & Company, 1992.

"The Grave Diggers or Robbery in the Northern Cemetery at New Albany," unpublished manuscript, Walter H. Kiser, New Albany Library Collection.

"Grave Robbers," *New Albany Ledger*, February 25, 1890.

"The Grave Robbers," *New Albany Ledger*, February 26, 1890.

"The Grave Robbery," *New Albany Ledger,* February 28, 1890.

"Grave Robbing," *New Albany Ledger*, March 1, 1890.

"Intimidating Ghastly Ghouls," *New Albany Ledger*, February 28, 1890.

"Ghoul Killed," *Louisville Courier-Journal*, February 25, 1890.

"The Graveyard Tragedy," *Louisville Courier-Journal*, February 25, 1890.

"Attempt in 1890 to Rob Graves Here Ended in Fatal Shooting," *New Albany Ledger-Tribune*, May 11,1958.

"Official Indictment: State of Indiana vs. James T. Blackburn, William E. Grant, and William Mukes." Floyd Circuit Court, May Term, 1890. Supplied by New Albany Public Library.

photo courtesy of Mark Marimen

The auditorium of the Rivoli Theater